Donald MacKenzie and The Murder Room

>>> This title is part of The Murder Room, our series dedicated to making available out-of-print or hard-to-find titles by classic crime writers.

Crime fiction has always held up a mirror to society. The Victorians were fascinated by sensational murder and the emerging science of detection; now we are obsessed with the forensic detail of violent death. And no other genre has so captivated and enthralled readers.

Vast troves of classic crime writing have for a long time been unavailable to all but the most dedicated frequenters of second-hand bookshops. The advent of digital publishing means that we are now able to bring you the backlists of a huge range of titles by classic and contemporary crime writers, some of which have been out of print for decades.

From the genteel amateur private eyes of the Golden Age and the femmes fatales of pulp fiction, to the morally ambiguous hard-boiled detectives of mid twentieth-century America and their descendants who walk our twenty-first century streets, The Murder Room has it all. >>>

The Murder Room
Where Criminal Minds Meet

themurderroom.com

T0352521

Donald MacKenzie 1908–1994

Donald MacKenzie was born in Ontario, Canada, and educated in England, Canada and Switzerland. For twenty-five years MacKenzie lived by crime in many countries. 'I went to jail,' he wrote, 'if not with depressing regularity, too often for my liking.' His last sentences were five years in the United States and three years in England, running consecutively. He began writing and selling stories when in American jail. 'I try to do exactly as I like as often as possible and I don't think I'm either psychopathic, a wayward boy, a problem of our time, a charming rogue. Or ever was.'

He had a wife, Estrela, and a daughter, and they divided their time between England, Portugal, Spain and Austria.

By Donald MacKenzie

Harry Calahan
Sahib from a Dead Man
Death Is a Friend
Sleep Is for the Rich

John Raven
Raven's Espionage
Raven in Flight
Raven and the Ratcatcher
Raven and the Kamikaze
Raven After Dark
Raven Settles a Score
Raven and the Paperhangers
Raven's Revenge
Raven, Come to the
Raven's Shadow
Nobody Here By That Name
A Savage Stay of Grace
by Any Illegal Means
Rogue Caution
The Eyes of the Goat
The Seed Deadly Sin

Standalone novels
Nowhere to Go
The Intruder
The Scent of Chance
Dangerous Silence
Epitaph
The Genial Stranger
Double Exposure
The Lonely Side of the River
One Sleep Between
Dead Straight
Three Minus Two
Night Boat from Puerto Vedra
The Kyle Contract
Postscript to a Dead Letter
The Singers and Collection
Deep, Dark and Dead
Cast of the Boundary

Raven and the Paperhangers

Donald MacKenzie

An Orion book

Copyright © The Estate of Donald MacKenzie 1980

The right of Donald MacKenzie to be identified as the author of this work has been asserted in accordance with the Copyright, Designs and Patents Act 1988.

This edition published by
The Orion Publishing Group Ltd
Orion House
5 Upper St Martin's Lane
London WC2H 9EA

An Hachette UK company
A CIP catalogue record for this book is available from the British Library

ISBN 978 1 4719 0509 4

www.orionbooks.co.uk

For Jo

Paperhanger: a forger; or one who passes bad paper money Partridge's *Dictionary of the Underworld*

ONE

THE FORD BLACK-AND-TAN STATION-WAGON was parked inconspicuously behind a PTT repair-truck. The two men sitting in the front of the car had a clear view of the main station entrance and were able to see right through into the concourse. It was ten minutes to two by the clock that was hanging there. Kent Tyler turned his wrist, checking the time against his watch. He was a big man with short steel-grey hair and black eyes and his blue flannel suit covered a well-conditioned body. Soft April rain had been falling most of the way in from Fontainebleau and the windscreen was spattered with drops. Tyler touched a switch on the dash, setting the wipers in motion.

'You understand that I don't want the guy near the house until we've seen what he's brought with him?'

Dark, longish hair and a thin high-bridged nose gave Rod de Wayne an air of raffish good breeding. He was wearing the collar of his shirt outside his sports jacket and a small gold lion was suspended from a chain around his neck. He swivelled his lean sun-tanned face towards his partner.

'Know something, Kent? You're getting paranoiac. Scotti's an organisation guy, an ace.'

'He's a convicted felon who was kicked out of the United States,' said Tyler. The windscreen was clean and he stopped the wipers.

De Wayne's grin revealed well-cared-for teeth. 'Come

off it, for fuck's sake! What do you care about his record?
You wanted the best man in the business and you've got
him.'

Tyler shrugged. Vegas had done more to Rod than give
him a sun-tan. Mixing with racketeers had given him a
kind of hip awareness. His eyes were never at rest, their
expression often at variance with the rest of his actor's face.
They had served together in Vietnam, Tyler captain to De
Wayne's lieutenant. The following years had sent them
in opposite directions but they kept up with one another.
'Birds of a feather', as their CO had said, not entirely without malice.

Tyler had reached his destination the previous autumn,
returning to the Karl Muellerstrasse apartment to find the
coop flown. A note from his wife, written on the office
stationery, was propped against the telephone.

DIDRIXON & LOEB INC.
NEW YORK, LONDON AND DUSSELDORF
INTERNATIONAL STOCKBROKERS

Kent:
By the time you read this Emma and I will be back in the
States. I've tried to ignore all the lying, cheating and
bullying for the sake of our daughter. I realise now that I
was wrong. By ignoring your behaviour I condoned it.
I shall be getting Mr Saunders to handle the divorce.
Please don't try to contact us and force me to do things
that I would only regret.

Natalie

He had read the note sourly. It was all there. The Yankee
self-righteousness, the characteristic threat at the end. Then
he'd gone out and got drunk. That was Friday night. He
was still drunk on Saturday, sitting alone in the apartment
with a half-empty bottle of rye and the pictures of his five-
year-old daughter. He'd finished the rye, burned the pictures
and gone to bed for twenty-four hours. That marked the

2

end of an era. The end of sex conferred as a goddam favour, a halt to the daily running arguments, the last of Natalie Coleman Tyler. The following Sunday he had driven from Düsseldorf to Winterberg and walked in the pine-woods. By the time he returned, his mind was made up. He planned his coup with the same mixture of audacity and ruthlessness that had put him in charge of the European office at the age of thirty-six. A young man in a hurry, as New York described him. Head Office liked to know about the domestic problems of their executives but Tyler managed to stifle the reasons for Natalie's defection. He explained her absence by saying that she had returned to the States to look for a school for Emma.

It had taken him the best part of a day to locate De Wayne playing straight man to a stand-up comic in a Vegas night-club. Tyler cabled expense money and De Wayne took the next flight to Germany. Tyler met him at Lohausen and they drove to a motel near Kreefeld. They had talked for most of the night, resuming their relationship as they had left it, tight in the way that only men who have held one another's lives in their hands can be. Tyler had explained his plan. Neither man wasted time with ethical implications. The only issue had been whether or not the scheme would work. De Wayne's racket friends in Vegas had given him the right contacts in Milan and he had flown on to Italy the following day. He was back again in a week, bringing a variety of forged identification papers and the promise of someone called Paolo Scotti.

Tyler glanced across at the concourse clock. The hand jerked past the hour. De Wayne dribbled cigarette smoke from the corner of his mouth, his eyes half-closed.

'I'd better make a move. The train's due in eight minutes.'

Tyler watched him into the railway-station. De Wayne moved like a dancer, his gait somewhere between a run and a lope. He was conscious of himself and of being observed.

Tyler lowered a window. The rain had stopped and what he wanted to do was stretch his legs. Caution kept him in the car. He had been careful to put himself on show as little as possible, constantly aware of the danger of a chance meeting with someone who knew him. It was difficult to think how he could have been more circumspect. He had waited for the New York auditors to make their annual visit before taking three weeks' holiday. There was nothing in the manner of his going or in its timing to alarm the Harvard Business School graduate who was waiting for the opportunity to step into Tyler's shoes. He left no un-finished business, no unresolved problems that could call for his intervention. Back in France, De Wayne and he moved into the rented hunting-lodge in the middle of Fontainebleau forest.

Tyler pitched his cigarette through the open window. De Wayne was making his way across to the car, flanked by a squat man in a light coat carrying a tartan holdall. Tyler shifted his seat, letting De Wayne in behind the wheel.

'Paolo Scotti,' said De Wayne.

The Italian reached forward from the rear seat and pushed out his hand. The backs of his fingers were furred with coarse black hair and he had snake's eyes in a pockmarked countenance. Thirty-five illegal years in the United States had given him a strong Brooklyn accent.

'Whadda you say, fella?'

Tyler felt a quick sense of outrage that he was actually sitting in a car with some greaseball who had been gaoled for forging dollar-bills.

'How was your trip?' he asked politely.

Scotti shrugged. 'Noise don't bother me. I sleep pretty good. You get those things I asked for?'

Three different firms had shipped the goods to Etampes. The Gronchi printing-press had come from Marseilles, car-boys of coloured inks from Strasbourg, the paper from Frankfurt. Tyler and De Wayne collected the merchandise in a rented pickup and took it to the *Pavillon Sarrault*.

'It's still in the crates,' said Tyler.

Scotti's teeth were streaked with nicotine stains. 'We got

4

things to show one another. I got mine in here.' He tapped the dispatch-case on the seat beside him.

Tyler took the bulky envelope from the glove-compartment. So far, the venture had cost him over forty thousand dollars. Five grand had gone to De Wayne for expenses. The printing-press and accessories had cost twenty thousand and there'd been rent on the two houses. Scotti wet his thumb and forefinger and riffled through the hundred-dollar bills. He looked up, satisfied.

'Sure enough, ten big ones.' He returned the envelope to Tyler and put his hand on his bag.

'Not here,' Tyler warned quickly. 'We'll go somewhere quiet.'

De Wayne already had the motor running. He snaked the big Ford through the circling taxis and headed west along boulevards that were drying under the fitful sun. Waiters were bustling out with chairs for the pavement tables. Glancing up at the rear-view mirror, Tyler found Scotti watching him. The Italian winked but Tyler took no notice. De Wayne's driving grew more fancy once they were near the Arc de Triomphe. He had been in Paris for three weeks and it showed. He drove like everyone else, bluffing and slamming on his brakes at the last moment. He turned into the Bois de Boulogne and down the Allée de Longchamp. There was a glimpse of well-accoutred horseback-riders cantering their mounts beneath chestnut trees that were fat with blossom. Soft rain had brought out the scents of spring, adding lustre to the green of the trees and the grass. The rails along the racetrack glittered white in the sunshine.

'Stop here,' Tyler said suddenly.

De Wayne trod on the brakes and killed the motor. There were no footpaths nearby and it was far too early for the car-borne hookers. The only person in sight was a painter on a derrick high against the stand on the far side of the track. De Wayne jammed his back against the door and stuck a cigarette in his mouth, watchful as Tyler extended a hand.

Scotti unfastened his bag with the air of a high-class

jeweller about to display a priceless diamond. Tyler laid the two bearer-bonds across his knees. His choice of General Chemical had been deliberate. They were blue-chip securities in the secondary money-market. This was a new issue, maturing in six years' time with a face value of five thousand dollars. The dividend coupons assured an eight-per-cent return on the investment. He held the bonds up to the light. Each showed the smoke-stack watermark used by General Chemical.

'How'd you manage that?' he asked quickly.

The Italian closed one eye. 'Magicians opened their mouths there'd be no more tricks.'

The bonds felt right, slightly greasy to the touch and the colours were perfectly matched. One was a forgery, the other he'd bought on the Düsseldorf stock-market. Looking down at them he was unable to detect which was which. For the first time he was really certain that this was going to work. Adrenalin raced but he hid his excitement. He brought his head up slowly.

'Are you sure you can do the serial numbers – I mean, perfectly?'

The Italian disposed of the question with a quick flick of his hairy fingers.

'You talk like a jerk, Mister. You tell me the numbers you want and you get 'em. I play a Gronchi press like Liberace does a piano.'

De Wayne took the bonds from Tyler's hand, shaking his head as he looked at them.

'What did I tell you?' he said admiringly.

Tyler's face showed none of his inner excitement. 'How about the plates?'

Scotti's fingers tapped the handle of his bag. 'I got 'em here. You oughta have paper enough for a run of six, seven hundred.'

'Five,' said Tyler. 'The figure was five hundred.'

Scotti bared stained teeth. 'I don't make no mistakes but I allow for them.' His hand swooped on the bonds. He selected one without hesitation and passed it to Tyler. 'This here's the kosher article. But you can bet your sweet ass General Chemical ain't gonna know the difference.'

Tyler gave him the ten thousand dollars. 'How long do you think it will take you to finish the run?'

Scotti scratched through the thin hair protecting his scalp. 'As long as I don't get no hassles it should be straightforward. Rod says we're out in the sticks somewhere?'

Tyler put the two bonds in the glove-compartment. 'We're in a forest forty-odd miles out of Paris. No neighbours and we're seven miles from the nearest town. There'll be no hassles.'

'I do my work right,' the Italian said. 'And I ain't breaking my ass for nobody.'

'Sure,' said Tyler. He was taking a strong dislike to Scotti. 'But you haven't told us how long it will take. Tomorrow? The next day? We have to know.'

Scotti thought for a moment. 'We can set up tonight. I'd say we oughta be through day after tomorrow. There's something else you ain't mentioned. I get ten per cent of the run.'

'Right,' said Tyler. De Wayne had made the arrangements necessary to get Scotti out of Milan.

The Italian shrugged. 'My business you don't deal with amateurs. It's something new for me. My business, everyone gets taken care of. Know what I mean?'

De Wayne laughed easily. 'What Paolo is saying is that everyone gets a piece of the action. His friends in Milan, my friends in Vegas.' Sudden alarm wiped the laughter from his face. Tyler followed his worried gaze. A car was parked about thirty yards away on the same side of the avenue. A couple of girls were leaning over the race-track rails as though watching the horses running. A third girl with honey-coloured hair and wearing a green dress was taking pictures of the two models with a long-lens camera. The station-wagon and its occupants were in her direct line of fire.

Tyler's stomach heaved. '*Shit!* How long have they been there?'

The Italian was already down on his knees behind the

7

front seat. De Wayne switched on and the motor caught. 'I don't know. I only just noticed them.'

'Switch that goddam thing off,' ordered Tyler. He felt now as if he'd been sandbagged. He wiped his dry forehead mechanically. 'We have to get that roll of film, Rod. We can't afford to be seen together.'

8

TWO

RAVEN WAS FIRST on to the escalator. His only baggage was a canvas shoulder-satchel containing a change of underclothes, his razor and toothbrush. It was almost a year now since he had met Kirstie Macfarlane. For the first frantic months they had wounded and forgiven quickly, probing one another's past until the agony of unshared experience gradually diminished. As Kirstie put it, what they had now was in no way inferior, it was different. They still lived together, sharing one another's life and home but with restated areas of independence. Both of them had the same readiness to give and unwillingness to take. Some of Raven's clothes were in Paris, some of Kirstie's on the Thames houseboat. One of her photographs had captured a thousand-dollar prize at the Venice Exhibition and this had meant new commissions. Raven respected her need to work and, in a sense, he envied it.

The Air France plane had left Heathrow under a light drizzle but by the time the bus arrived at the Gare des Invalides terminal, the sun was out. He saw Kirstie waiting at the top of the escalator, peering down, one hand holding her honey-coloured hair out of her eyes. A light trenchcoat was thrown around her shoulders. Her face lit up as she saw him and she was in his arms. She stepped back, shaking her head at his sneakers, jeans and wind-cheater.

'I wonder you don't get busted on sight,' she said. '*I'd* bust you if I worked for Customs! You look like some drop-out making his first hash run!'

He steered her towards the exit. There was no sign of her car outside.

She answered his unvoiced question, hanging on tightly to his arm. 'It just wasn't worth it. Parking places on the island are at a premium.'

The cabs were arriving in rapid succession. Their driver turned out to be an axe-faced woman who accepted their destination and company without any comment. Raven dug into the shoulder-satchel and produced a four-ounce bottle of *Paco Rabanne*. She put it away in her purse, smiling vaguely.

'Your enthusiasm overwhelms me,' he said sarcastically.

She dug deeper into his arm. 'I was thinking,' she said. 'I'm sorry.'

He lit a duty-free Gitane, savouring the first inhalation with the old belief that the cigarette was different from the Gitanes sold in England. Kirstie loved Paris and its people. They had style, she said. The girls with their chic legs and bottoms, the traffic-cops with their capes and Errol Flynn moustaches. Even the flat-footed waiter at the *Dome* with his warts and flatulence had style according to Kirstie. But the French made Raven uneasy. Beyond the Latin charm and *gamine* comradeship, he saw a series of cash-registers recording the monetary profit of any given moment. Paris, in his book, was a commercialised city with no place for someone like him.

Kirstie spoke. He turned his head. 'Jerry and Louise? They're all right, I suppose. I mean, it's a strange thing to ask considering you saw them only ten days ago.'

Her fingers fiddled nervously with the wristband of her blue-dialled watch. She was wearing the garnet cluster that he had given her on the third finger of her left hand. The watch and the ring were the only jewellery that she possessed, or at any rate wore. She made it plain that she wanted no more. Her mother's engagement ring had been in the bank vault for more than ten years.

'There's something on your mind,' he challenged. 'What is it?'

She shook her head. The cab swung east on to Boulevard St Germain and the sudden lurch brought their bodies close together. He felt the tenseness in her and wrapped an arm around her shoulders, ignoring the sardonic grin in the driving-mirror.

'Tell me,' he said with his lips in her hair. 'Is it Madame Frontenac again?'

Irma Frontenac was a picture-dealer who lived on the floor beneath Kirstie. She was a harridan with cocaine-ravaged nostrils who was given to malicious scandal. Kirstie freed herself gently.

'I'll tell you later,' she said.

The taxi stopped on Quai d'Anjou. A wicket was set in the heavy doors opposite. The seventeenth-century building soared six storeys, crowded in on each side by its neighbours like a dowager on a ballroom chair. Kirstie pressed the bell and the wicket buzzed open. The small woman standing outside the *loge* had neat grey hair and the suspicious eyes of her calling. For some unvoiced reason Raven was one of her favourites and she smiled welcome.

'*Bonjour, Monsieur!* So once again you escape from the fogs of London!'

He embroidered the running joke in his fluent French. 'Evidently, Madame. It is impossible at the moment to walk the streets there without a lantern.' He handed her a cello-phane-wrapped package from his satchel.

She sniffed at the kippers with delight, dislodging the fat cur behind her with a swift backward kick. It was an un-prepossessing animal that spent much time stinking out the doorways. It ran now squealing.

The *concierge* was suddenly coy. '*Merci beaucoup, Monsieur!*' A childless widow, her dual interests were interfering in the lives of her tenants and enforcing the house-rules. It was a communal property with each tenant con-tributing towards the service charges. Madame Rambert ran a tight ship, offering advice or criticism according to whim. She was capable of genuine charity and had once emptied a pail of water over a Senator found without excuse on the premises. She cocked her head on one side, a sure sign that she was about to be humorous.

'It is just as well that Monsieur is in Paris again. Mademoiselle has been seeing ghosts, I fear.'

Kirstie spoke in English. 'I don't want to talk about it in front of her.' She hurried up the steps.

Madame Rambert's tone was confidential. 'Rest assured, Monsieur. There have been no strangers in the building.'

He followed Kirstie through the glass doors. 'Old hag,' she said viciously. 'You should have given the scent to her. God knows she needs it.'

He pressed the button and the elevator shuddered down from the upper floors. The interior of the cage was quilted in faded velvet that was rubbed and greasy from wear. A mirror offered a disconcerting full-length reflection. There was just enough room for two people to stand facing one another. The cage ascended briskly through the lower floors, losing momentum as it approached the top of the shaft. Raven stepped out gratefully. He had a constant fear of being trapped inside the eighty-year-old device.

Kirstie's apartment was reached through a fine carved door. Servants had slept there once, shuttling between the attics and downstairs rooms. The apartment had been converted with the flair that the French have for clothing history with comfort. Kirstie had bought the place from a Surrealist painter who had broken through the ceiling into a forgotten loft. He had turned the space into a vast studio and added balconies to the dormer windows. A circular iron staircase connected the studio with the two bedrooms, kitchen and bathroom below. Raven shut the front door. There was a sense of isolation up here, of space and security. The apartment gave him the same feeling that he had on his houseboat. Large shuttered windows let in light on exposed beams and whitewashed walls. Pewter plates brightened the dark Breton dresser. Patchwork quilts made by Kirstie's grandmother covered the beds. Animal prints and engravings hung on the walls. The converted loft was used as Kirstie's studio and drawing-room. Its size swallowed the white-painted bookshelves, her record collection and hi-fi set. Photographic equipment filled two large closets. The pine floor was polished and strewn with rugs. There was an open fireplace where logs burned in the winter.

Raven pulled out the last of his duty-free buys, a litre bottle of malt whisky that he placed on the dresser. An earthenware bowl was filled with his favourite apples. He bit into one, speaking with his mouth full.

'OK, let's have it. What's troubling you?'

She hung her Burberry on a stand in the hallway and sat down at the kitchen table, holding her face in her hands.

'This isn't going to work, you know.'

'Cut the crap and get on with it,' he said.

She looked up. 'Can you remember me telling you about a job I had to do for some people called Sandler Scarves?'

'How could I forget?' he answered, smiling. 'A thousand dollars for an hour or so's work!' The commission had been one of those that came from her Venice award and he had been impressed.

She glanced at her nails. Handling cameras constantly, she kept them short.

'Sandler's bright. He knew exactly what he wanted for *Vogue*. He needed something chic and sporty. You know the kind of thing, elegant young Paris with the wind in its hair.'

He kept his face dead-pan. 'How about the stern of a boat? That way you'd get the smell of the engine as well as the wind in your hair.'

She looked at him with contempt. 'I hate it when you try to be funny. You're just not equipped for it. Anyway, the session was scheduled for yesterday. The agency sent a couple of models around and they got here about ten. I was driving them out to Longchamp.'

She paused as though expecting some comment. 'Wizard,' was all he said.

She blew hard, shaking her head. 'It was raining when they got here so we sat around drinking coffee and waiting for the weather to clear. The sun did finally come out and we drove to Longchamp. The kids put on the scarves and I started firing away. I must have shot three rolls of film when I noticed this station-wagon in the background. I was using a long lens and the three men in the car were right in my line of fire. I kept on pressing the button. The car seemed to add a touch of verisimilitude.'

'I like it,' he said reflectively. 'An ace word. Veri-simili-tude!'

She waited until his face had sobered. 'Anyway the men must have noticed that I'd seen them. The one at the wheel was pointing across at us while the guy in back had ducked down behind the front seat.'

'He probably slipped,' said Raven.

'You might not find the rest of this quite so amusing,' Kirstie warned quietly. 'The third man got out of the car and came over to where we were standing. He spoke to me, ignoring the girls. He wanted to know if I understood English. He was an American, well-dressed and well-mannered. He asked if I were a professional photographer. When I told him yes, he asked for my business card. He had a friend in the rag-trade, he said. Someone who needed work done.'

Raven stifled a yawn. 'So he called you last night and sex reared its ugly head.'

'Wrong again,' she said, shaking her hair back. 'In any case there was nothing suggestive about his manner.'

Raven put his hand on his heart. 'I do apologise.'

'Do you want to hear the rest of this or not?' she demanded.

'I do, I do,' he said quickly.

'It was late when I got home last night,' she said. 'It must have been well after midnight. I'd been out to supper with Sara Weekes. Anyway I went to sleep almost immediately. I don't know what it was that woke me but I knew instinct-ively that someone had been in the room.'

He looked at her questioningly. 'How do you mean, you *knew*?'

She shifted her weight on to her elbows. 'I smelled him, that's how. He was wearing a very distinctive cologne. I could hear him tiptoeing up the stairs to the studio. I lay there absolutely petrified, too scared to move, even. I could hear his shoes squeaking, the reflection of his flashlight on the ceiling in the hallway.'

Her voice was calm and she was half-smiling but he realised that she was still scared. The knowledge angered him. He reached across the table and took her hands in his.

'Was anything stolen?'

She moved her head from side to side. 'Not a thing. I checked, of course. But he'd been through every drawer in the desk, searched all through the papers and opened all the cupboards. Come with me. I want to show you something!'

He followed her up the circular staircase. Afternoon sunshine was streaming through the dormer windows, slanting across the polished boards between the Afghan rugs. Kirstie pointed down at the floor. There was a clear impression of a ribbed rubber sole.

'Just take a look at that!'

The print was of a man's right shoe, made as its wearer approached the painted desk. Raven looked for more prints but found none. Except in the one instance, the intruder had kept to the floor-rugs.

'Why didn't you use the phone, call the police?' asked Raven.

She looked at him steadily. 'I tried to. It was dark, remember, and I was scared. I couldn't even remember the number. Whoever it was, he must have heard me pick up the phone. The extension up here tinkles when you call from the bedroom.'

'Go on,' said Raven.

'I heard him coming down again, then the front door opened and shut very quietly. I didn't hear the elevator. He must have gone down the stairs. A car drove off just as I got to the window.'

'But you didn't actually *see* anyone?'

She shook her head. 'I didn't have to see him. I heard him and I smelled him.'

15

He wrapped an arm around her, holding her tight. 'What happened to the pictures you took?'

She wriggled out of his embrace. 'For God's sake stop treating me as if I were some hysterical maid.'

'What happened to the pictures?' he repeated.

'They're at *Foto-St-Louis*,' she answered. 'Just around the corner. They do all my processing.'

He looked around the sunlit studio. 'And you're absolutely sure that nothing is missing?'

Her look was assured. 'I'm positive. And I made a point of asking Madame Rambert if she'd heard someone leaving the building late. I complained about the noise of the car. She said that she had heard nothing but in any case she'd have been asleep by then.'

'Right,' he said and shrugged. 'It doesn't really matter whether or not she heard. It's no trick to get in or out of the building. Let's take a look at your front door.'

The apartment was the only one on the top floor and the stair-carpet was thick. None of the other tenants would hear an intruder creeping downstairs at one o'clock in the morning. There were two locks on Kirstie's front door, a mortise and a Yale. Raven bent down, inspecting the edge of the door. He straightened his back again.

'Was the mortise on last night?'

Her face coloured. 'I forgot.'

'Forgot,' he said scathingly. 'How many times do I have to tell you that this door's an invitation to a burglar if you don't use the mortise! Your Aunt Fanny could open it with a plastic playing-card. Look at these scratch-marks on the paint. The guy probably used a match-box.'

'I'm sorry,' she said quietly.

'You could be raped or killed,' he said. 'Any night of the week! Imagine what the police are going to say when they hear that you've got a mortise-lock, a burglar-chain and two bolts and that you don't use any of them. You're crazy, that's what!'

She wriggled a shoulder and muttered something that he didn't hear. They went down to the kitchen. She shifted the duty-free scotch from one side of the dresser to the other, her face still red. It was the kind of territorial marking that she still made with inanimate objects, removing things from where he had placed them. She did it without offence, almost mindlessly, and he kept his irritation to himself, aware of his own idiosyncrasies.

Standing at the window, he glanced down at the street below. Kirstie's Chrysler was parked in the middle of a long line of vehicles. Fishermen were casting their lines from the parapet beyond. From what he had seen, their usual catch was about the size of a sardine and the colour of mud. The Seine was swifter and greener than the Thames but he preferred his own river.

He turned and saw her across the hallway in the bedroom, brushing her hair with long steady strokes.

'We'll have to go to the police,' he said.

She suspended her brushing. 'Why?'

'Why?' he repeated. She disliked all forms of bureaucracy but this was ridiculous. 'Look, Kirstie. A man has broken into your apartment. The fact that nothing was stolen is beside the point. Are you listening to what I am saying?'

'I'm listening.' She smiled at him across the hallway. 'I've missed you, sweetheart!'

He walked to her, lifted her chin and forced her to look at him. 'You're acting very strangely and it worries me. What time are your films supposed to be ready?'

'At six o'clock, why?'

His eyes sought the dressing-table. 'Where is the claim-tag?'

'Here.' She opened a drawer. 'It was in the pocket of my Burberry, hanging in the clothes-closet. He must have gone through my purse before he went upstairs. The zip was left open.'

His fingers closed on the claim-tag. 'I'll take this,' he said easily.

The splotches of freckles were vivid against her pale skin. 'I can see where you could get to be a pain in the ass, John Raven.'

17

He heard her with half an ear, thinking about the films she had shot. 'We can blow those pictures up and find out what is making our friends so nervous. Meanwhile back at the ranch . . .' He grinned.

The hand holding the hair-brush lowered slowly. 'Yes?'

'We go to bed,' he said.

He turned over, waking from a dream in which strangers eyed him from doorways. The curtains were closed but there was enough light to see Kirstie's eyes. She had removed her wrist-watch and her body was white against the patch-work quilt. A vague memory persisted in his brain and he pushed up on an elbow.

'Did I hear the phone ringing?'

'That was nearly an hour ago.' She ruffled his hair. 'You've been asleep since then, my darling.'

He reached for his shorts and sat on the side of the bed with his long legs dangling. It was half past four by the bedside clock. He showered, washing his hair with her shampoo, and then put on his clothes again. He opened the curtains, letting in the last of the April afternoon. Kirstie shielded her eyes from the sudden light and lay across the bed, relaxed and unwilling to move. Their sex life had lost none of its vigour. He walked back to the window. All the rooms except the studio overlooked the street. It had rained since they had gone to bed and the car roofs were glistening.

He yawned. 'Who was it called?'

She stretched one leg after another, shaking each as a cat does. 'Some man. A wrong number. He hung up as soon as I answered.'

Raven turned, combing through wet hair with his fingers. 'It's odds-on it was your visitor from last night, casing the joint.'

She frowned. 'Ouch! You really think so?'

He dried the back of his neck. 'You're damn right I think so. He's a persistent bugger. Where did you say the photographer was?'

She sat up, exposing firm bare breasts. 'Just around the corner. Near the post-office.'

'How well do you know the guy, the photographer?'

She looked at him quaintly. 'I don't understand.'

'It's perfectly simple,' he answered. 'I asked how well you know the guy.' The Ile-St-Louis was a strange place in many respects, in the heart of the city yet necessarily cut-off because of its clannishness. The inhabitants tended to inter-marry and many of the businesses on the island had been in the same family for two or more centuries.

Kirstie shook her head, her smile indulgent. 'I do believe you're jealous. David's just a friend who happens to be very good at his job.'

'I'm going out,' Raven said shortly. 'I won't be long.'

She swung her legs to the floor. 'Suppose the phone rings again. What should I do?'

'Answer it,' he said. 'It might be another admirer.' He ducked the pillow she threw and let himself out of the apartment.

Madame Rambert waved as he crossed the courtyard. The nearest Métro station was on the Right Bank. People who lived on the island were crossing the bridge, returning from work. Raven turned right instead of following Kirstie's direction. Once around the corner, he sprinted hard, slow-ing as he neared Rue St Louis-en-l'Isle. There were customers sitting outside the café. This was Raven's eleventh visit in a year and some of the people he knew by sight. None of the others looked suspicious. A red cross identified the drug-store. He crossed the street to *Foto-St-Louis*. The store was fitted in modern French style with the accent on chrome and plate-glass. An ingenious arrangement of strobes and cut-outs in the window simulated a torrid beach in Guada-loupe. Nut-brown bodies reclined under reed shelters.

Raven pushed the door and a buzzer sounded. A youngish man came through a door behind the counter. The room looked like a dark-room. He was wearing a high-necked white nylon smock and his hair was short and blond. Expensive cameras were displayed on the shelves behind

19

him. Raven introduced himself. David offered a friendly smile.

'*Bonsoir, Monsieur*. Mademoiselle Macfarlane has spoken to me of you.'

Raven put the claim-tag on the counter. 'Is this stuff ready?'

The Frenchman smiled and opened a drawer. He produced three yellow folders.

'You know, Monsieur, Mademoiselle Macfarlane is a very good photographer. I would dare to say talented.'

Raven had the first piece of film-strip in his hand when the door to the street was opened. The newcomer's ear-length dark hair, sun-tanned face and thin beak of a nose gave him the look of an Indian brave. He nodded pleasantly at Raven who snapped the rubber band back on the folders. Kirstie had described the man who had spoken to her in the Bois as having steel-grey hair. The stranger's accent confirmed his nationality.

'Do you speak English?'

'Yes,' said Raven.

'Does he?' The other man's teeth were well-kept.

'I doubt it,' said Raven. 'Maybe I can help. What is it you want?'

'Just a roll of film. Thirty-five millimetre, black and white.' The American was wearing a small gold lion on a chain about his neck. Raven glanced down at the man's feet. His wingtip shoes had rubber soles. Raven translated the American's request and David produced the roll of film. The American paid and left. The top of his head showed as he walked up the street. Raven paid his bill and pushed the yellow folders back across the counter.

'I'm in a bit of a rush. I wonder if you'd mind dropping these off at Mademoiselle Macfarlane's place. You can leave them with the concierge.'

David swept the folders into a drawer. 'No trouble at all. I'll do it on my way home.'

The smell of freshly ground coffee was strong on the street outside. Smoke-grey clouds drifted across the reddening sky. Raven started back towards the river, wondering how best he might get Kirstie on a plane to the Greek islands. He needed a couple of weeks alone there with her, before the influx of tourists destroyed the peace of deserted beaches. He wanted to bake potatoes in a driftwood fire, climb the dried-up arroyos strewn with the debris of spring torrents. Most of all he wanted to be alone with her and talk. The problem was going to be getting her away from her work. She had increased her charges but the work kept coming in.

He turned right on to Quai d'Anjou. A stationary Peugeot with two wheels up on the kerb forced him to slow. As he drew abreast of the doorway, the American he had seen earlier stepped from a doorway. He yanked the rear door of the car open, completely blocking Raven's passage.

'In !' he ordered, smiling for the benefit of anyone watching. Then his shoulder toppled Raven into the rear of the Peugeot. The door banged shut and the car accelerated, slamming Raven back hard against the upholstery. His abductor was holding a short-barrelled Smith & Wesson thirty-eight. He was still smiling. No one on the street had noticed the incident. There were no shouts of alarm, no attempts to stop the car that was speeding towards the Left Bank. The thirty-eight was jammed into Raven's ribs. All he could see of the driver was a pair of well-tailored shoulders and the back of a prematurely white head. This couple must have been watching the apartment. The man with the gun had followed him into the photographer's.

The Peugeot crossed Boulevard St Michel and climbed the labyrinth of narrow streets below the Panthéon. It stopped in a tiny square where wet washing hung outside paint-blistered shutters. A statue dribbled in the middle of a slimy fountain. Pavement and cobblestones were covered with pigeon-droppings. The driver cut the motor and turned in his seat. He looked to be in his middle thirties and was wearing wraparound sunglasses.

De Wayne's hand shot out, clicking thumb against finger. 'OK, friend, I'll take those photographs.'

Raven cleared his throat. The street was empty. 'What photographs? What is this, anyway?'

Seen closer, De Wayne's eyes were flecked with yellow like a cat's. 'The rolls of film, asshole!'

Raven shook his head cautiously. 'I left them there. Some of the prints had blemishes. The man's going to do them over again.' His neck was stiff and he could only look in one direction, straight ahead at the dashboard. The ignition key was in the lock. A second key dangled from a ring bearing a small plastic label. Printed in white-on-blue was the legend RENTED FROM SHELL-SULLY-LA-FORET.

De Wayne poked the Smith & Wesson into Raven's ribs. 'Get your jacket off!' He handed the gun to the driver and started searching Raven's clothing. No space or aperture that might have concealed the film strip of prints was missed. He made the Englishman take off his shoes and felt in his underwear. He straightened up with a puzzled expression.

'The bastard's clean. Nothing.'

Raven's head was down, legs apart, hands resting on his knees. He could see the ribbing on De Wayne's rubber sole. It was the same pattern as the footprint left in the studio. The door opened suddenly and a powerful shove propelled him sideways out of the car. His belongings landed on the cobblestones beside him. The Peugeot kicked dust in his face and reared away. Still on his knees, he started picking up money, keys and lighter under the interested stare of a woman who had appeared at a nearby window. She raised her forearms comfortably on a cushion and was joined by a cat. Raven followed the dwindling sound of the Peugeot as far as a corner café where he bought a *jeton* for the payphone. The number listed for *Foto-St-Louis* failed to answer. He tried the number given for the proprietor's home address and was luckier.

'This is Mademoiselle Macfarlane's friend,' Raven said hurriedly. The photographer spoke with his mouth full. 'It is already done, Monsieur. Half an hour ago.'

Raven hung up and walked till he found a cab. The way

back to Quai d'Anjou took him past the photography store. The window was lit but the place looked firmly closed. He paid off the hack and buzzed the *loge*. Madame Rambert emerged, holding up the three yellow envelopes. He stuffed them in a pocket. She looked at him curiously.

'Is there something wrong, Monsieur?'

'Nothing,' he said, and hurried through the glass doors into the lobby. He pushed the top-floor lift button, but the cage started to descend again before he could get out. The cocaine-sniffer from below had pressed the call-button. She was wearing a fringed shawl around her bony shoulders and her hair was an alarming shade of red. The mouth she had painted only vaguely approximated the true shape of her lips. He opened the cage. It was the fifth time she had done this to him and his voice was weary.

'Why don't you let me get out before you press the button, Madame?'

She bridled with indignation, her deep voice booming out of her raddled countenance.

'How dare you adopt that tone with me, Monsieur! I will have you know that you are addressing a lady!'

'I'm glad to hear it,' he said. 'You don't have much else left.' He moved away before she could answer and climbed the last flight of stairs to let himself into the apartment. Kirstie was peeling mushrooms at the kitchen table and wearing a Victorian nightgown. A couple of steaks covered with coarse black pepper were on a wooden platter in front of her and she had carried the portable television set in from the bedroom. There was a picture on the screen but the sound was off. He dropped the photographs on the table and poured himself a large scotch and water.

'I've just been had,' he announced.

She glanced across at the yellow folders. 'If you're talking about the bill, quality work is expensive. I'll give you your money back. There's no reason why you should pay for my developing.'

He shook his head. 'I'm not talking about money. Can you imagine it? I've just been pulled into a car and searched, then thrown out like a bag of rubbish!'

She put the knife down very carefully, wide-eyed as she sought his face. 'You're putting me on! I don't believe it!'

He moved his hand from side to side. 'I am *not* putting you on! It was your friends all right. One of them followed me into the photographer's to make sure where the pictures were. I had an odd feeling the moment I saw him and as soon as he left I gave the films back to David. I asked him to leave them with Madame Rambert. A couple of minutes later they jumped me just around the corner.'

She pushed the bowl of mushrooms aside, her gaze worried. 'You're hurt!' she said anxiously.

'Only my ego.' He took a gulp of the scotch and water. 'In broad daylight no less! It's outrageous. I'm going to teach these bastards a lesson. They just can't get away with it.'

'How?' she asked. She scratched her nose with the knife-handle. 'I mean, how are you going to teach them a lesson?'

But Raven wasn't listening. 'It wasn't a station-wagon they were driving, either. They were in a rented Peugeot. Turn that thing off!' He gestured at the television set. 'I'm trying to think. We'll take a look at these for a start.'

He picked the yellow folders from the table and they went up to the studio. He drew the curtains while Kirstie opened the closet where she kept her photographic equipment. She took out her film-strip viewer. The first frame showed the two models striking elegant poses on the race-track rails.

'Skip those!' Raven said impatiently. 'Get to the ones with the car.'

Kirstie sorted through the film-strips. Eight frames featured the station-wagon and its three occupants. The vehicle was a seventy-eight Ford with German plates.

'DU,' said Raven. 'That's a Düsseldorf registration.' He adjusted the focus and bent lower. Two men were sitting in front, half-turned to face the man in the back. All three appeared to be deep in conversation. Another shot showed them staring directly into the camera, surprise and alarm showing on their faces. In the last frame, the white-haired man was out of the car and crossing the grass towards Kirstie.

'Hold it!' said Raven. 'That's enough.' Kirstie glanced across at him expectantly as he opened the curtains. He used her shears to snip the eight frames from the film-strip and put them in an envelope. 'I'll hang on to these.'

'The agency might want them,' she ventured.

'Pictures of a station-wagon?' He made a face. 'What on earth for?'

She sounded doubtful. 'Are you sure that those men are the same ones who attacked you?'

'I'm sure,' he said grimly. He was still smarting from the indignity of the experience. He addressed the envelope to himself care of the American Express Company on the Rue Scribe.

Kirstie bent down, putting the viewer back in the closet. The blonde hair on the nape of her neck grew in soft tendrils. 'I wish I knew why this sort of thing always seems to happen to us,' she said.

'We don't pray enough,' he said shortly. He licked a stamp and stuck it on the envelope.

They went down to the kitchen again. Kirstie pulled the tab on a can of Coke and straddled a chair by the window. She spoke with a foam moustache on her upper lip.

'You know what doesn't make sense? Why are these people behaving so mysteriously? I mean, I'd have given them the pictures if I'd known that they wanted them.'

'Come off it,' he said with sudden exasperation. 'What do you think this is? Look, I've no more idea than you who these characters are, but this much I do know – they've broken in here and they've pulled a gun on me. Now that means business, Kirstie. People like that aren't about to come sidling up, tipping their hats and asking for favours.'

She used her foot to depress the pedal on the garbage-container and dropped the Coke can inside. She stared out of the window and he followed her gaze. There was no sign of the Peugeot below but he hadn't expected that there would be.

'So what are we going to do?' she asked.

'We're going to the police, of course!'

Her chair-legs scraped closer to the table. 'I'd rather not go to the police,' she said.

He cocked his head. 'Oh really? Then what do you suggest?'

She shrugged, avoiding his questioning look. 'Now wait a minute,' he said. 'Let's get this absolutely straight. You say you don't want to go to the police. Why?'

She moved her shoulders once more. 'Do I always have to give a reason? Can't I just say for once that I don't want to do something, period?'

'No,' he said. 'You can't. I come over from London to pass a couple of quiet days, enjoyable days. I find you acting strangely and the first news I get is that you have been burgled. Next thing I know, the burglars pull me off the street in broad daylight, search me and dump me. Right?'

'Yes.' Her voice was very quiet.

'Thank you,' he said sarcastically. She was listening with her eyes closed and the pose irritated him. 'Then you ask me what we're going to do. Go to the police, I say. Any normal person would say the same. But not you apparently.'

She opened her eyes. 'I have my reasons.'

'Then would you mind telling me what they are?' he demanded.

Her mouth was still obstinate. 'OK,' he said. 'Let's try another tack. You asked me what we were going to do. What did you expect me to say?'

She gave him look for look. 'I'll tell you what I expected. I expected sensitivity. I should have known better.'

'What utter crap!' he exploded. He laughed and shook his head. 'Come now, Kirstie, you'll have to do better than that.'

'OK,' she said in a tight voice. 'You want the facts, of course. You don't want to hear about feelings.'

'Jesus,' he said resignedly. 'I don't know whether I'm coming or going here. The one thing I certainly don't want are riddles. *Why don't you want to go to the police?*'

She drew a figure on the table-top with her finger. 'Have it your way. I didn't want to tell you all this. I'm a Canadian working in France, right?'

'Right,' he agreed cautiously.

She suspended her doodling. 'My last work-permit expired this week. What happens is that you take your renewal application to your local police-station. They have to give you a clearance. You know the sort of thing, that you're a person of good reputation, no police-record.'

He nodded. 'So? Where's the problem?'

'The man I had to deal with at the police-station. He's the problem.' Her hair-ribbon matched the colour of her eyes exactly.

He thought that he saw a glimmer of light. 'You mean that you didn't get your permit. You're working illegally. Is that what you're trying to say?'

She moved her heard from side to side. 'I was a couple of days getting in my application. All right – I know I was careless. I forgot and that's all there is to it. Anyway, the person I had to see was someone new. A new Commissaire who had just taken over. A horrible man called Suzini. I sensed that something was wrong the moment I entered his office. A woman is aware of these things. He made a point of leaving the door open. That struck me as odd for a start. He spoke very quietly. He made it perfectly plain that because I was late he didn't have to process my application.'

'That's nonsense,' said Raven. 'A pure technicality.'

'I'm telling you exactly what happened,' she insisted. 'He mentioned this Australian girl who'd had the same difficulty but they'd become friends. She got her permit. OK, he was trying it on but the message was clear.'

'Then what?'

Her fingers were still moving. 'He asked me what sort of pictures I took. Whether I ever did nudes. He wanted to know if I lived alone. It was horrid. Not so much the things he said as the way he said them. He kept looking at me in

27

this very strange way. I was scared and humiliated. He made me feel dirty.'

Anger flared in his mind. He knew the type. Renegade cops who threw men in gaol and then visited their wives or girlfriends offering favour for favour.

'And you just sat there, taking it all?'

'That's right,' she admitted. 'I acted dumb, pretending that I didn't understand. In the end he got quite angry. He stamped my application but I knew I'd made an enemy.'

'The bastard!' Raven said with feeling. 'Didn't you complain to anyone?'

'Like who?' she demanded. 'And what would I say? I told you, the door was open all the time and he never as much touched my hand. I was just happy to get out of there. I talked to a couple of people on the island since and it seems that Suzini has a name as a lady's man.'

He thought for a moment. He had never been a jealous man and what he was feeling now was ridiculous. Yet it was none the less real for being without foundation.

'OK,' he said. 'We'll file our complaints somewhere else. In another district.'

'That won't work either,' she said quickly. 'We're living in the Fourth Arondissement and that's where everything happened. No matter where we went they'd refer us back to Suzini.'

'And you don't want to face him? Then I'll go alone.'

'No,' she said quickly. 'If you go, I'm going too.'

'I have to do something,' he answered. 'You've got your permit and I can't let these clowns walk all over us.'

She lifted her arms and let them fall. 'Whatever you say. Do you want to eat now or what?'

'No, later,' he said. 'You'd better put your clothes on. And for once, let me do the talking. In any case, my French is better than yours.'

She disappeared into the bedroom to make her usual rapid change and emerged wearing a yellow dress and sandals with a scarf around her hair. She gave him his passport. He glanced down at it.

'What's this for?'

'Well, for one thing you're a foreigner,' she said. 'And the police may well ask to see your passport. That old bag downstairs will have told them that you're staying here.'

He looked at her curiously. Bitchiness wasn't her field in general. 'Are you saying that Madame Rambert's a police-informer?'

'Of course.' She slung the strap of her purse over her shoulder. 'Cab-drivers and *concierges*, they're all narks in Paris. I'd have thought that you would have known that.'

The streets were gleaming and fresh-smelling. They walked west on Rue St Louis-en-l'Isle and crossed the bridge. Tourists were posing in front of Nôtre Dame. The flower-sellers' stands were a riot of colour. A shield bearing the arms of the Republic distinguished the seventeenth-century building from its neighbours. They passed an armed police-man on the steps and went along the corridor. It was the first time that Raven had been in a French police-station but much about it was familiar. There was the same smell of human sweat, stale cigarette-smoke and disinfectant, the same shabby furniture scarred with butt-burns, the same purposeful movements of hard-eyed men with a contempt for civilians.

A uniformed cop was sitting at a table near half-glass doors that led into a large room with desks. The clatter of typewriters mingled with the sound of men's voices. Kirstie sank on to a bench, ostentatiously avoiding contact with the greasy wall. She lit a cigarette and crossed her legs. Raven explained himself to the man in uniform. He had been assaulted earlier and dragged into a car by a couple of men he had never seen before. They were foreigners, he said. Americans by their speech and clothes.

The cop listened with one finger hooked around a tooth. He removed the finger and spat, unclear about Raven's reasons for being in the commissariat.

'You wish to file a complaint, Monsieur?'

'That's right,' said Raven. He had a sudden feeling that his sneakers and jeans were not creating too good an impression. 'I'd like to speak to someone in authority,' he added.

The policeman's chin lifted. 'I *am* someone in authority.'

'I mean someone in the detective branch,' said Raven.

The officer dropped his pen as though it had stung him. He looked Raven up and down, spat again and thrust out his hand, snapping his fingers.

'Papers!'

Raven felt for his passport. A man in plain clothes was standing behind the glass, watching. Raven gave his passport to the cop, who flicked through the title pages and looked at Raven's photograph, grunting. He no longer made a pretence at civility. 'Where do you live?'

'Quai d'Anjou,' answered Raven. 'One hundred thirty-seven.'

The glass door opened. The uniformed officer rose and saluted the plain-clothes man. The newcomer was slovenly dressed in a suit mapped with gravy stains. His hand-knitted cardigan was inches longer than his jacket. He was about fifty with cheeks that folded over on themselves like those of a bloodhound. Kirstie's face tightened. The plain-clothes man had a word with his subordinate and looked at Kirstie as though noticing her for the first time.

'*Bonsoir, Mademoiselle!*'

Kirstie's answer was guarded. '*Bonsoir, Monsieur.*'

The man turned toward Raven. 'I am Commissaire Suzini. The officer tells me that you have a problem?'

Raven nodded. Suzini matched Kirstie's description.

'Follow me, if you please, M'sieu, 'dame.' He opened a door on an airless room with bars and wire mesh at the windows. The only furniture was a table and stool. A pad of clean white paper and a pen were neatly ranged on the table. Suzini closed the door.

'Sit, Mademoiselle,' he said, indicating the stool. Kirstie took the seat, her eyes warning Raven. Suzini had Raven's passport in his hand.

'Now, Monsieur, what is your difficulty?'

The walls of the building were thick. It was quiet in the room. A man locked in here, thought Raven, facing the blank paper and pen, would feel a hypnotic wish to unburden himself.

'Well,' Raven said cautiously. 'As I explained to the other officer. A couple of men dragged me into a car not much more than an hour ago. One of them had previously broken into Miss Macfarlane's apartment.'

'Indeed?' Suzini pursed his lips. 'An hour ago, you say? Were you injured?'

'No,' said Raven. He knew what was coming.

'Then what kept you?' Suzini's smile was a withdrawal of lips from nicotine-stained teeth.

'It happened at the corner of the Quai d'Anjou,' Raven said doggedly. 'They were Americans. I managed to get the number of their car.'

The Commissioner was unimpressed. 'And the burglary, when was that?'

'The night before last.'

'And you wait until now to report it?'

'Miss Macfarlane wanted to talk to me first.'

Suzini nodded heavily. 'She needed your advice, no doubt. On how to report a burglary. And what did these American burglars steal?'

'Nothing,' said Raven. 'And there was only one burglar.'

'Nothing,' Suzini repeated sarcastically.

'That's beside the point, surely,' said Raven. 'I have the registration number of the car they were driving this afternoon. The sooner those are on the air, the sooner we'll nail them.'

Suzini's head tilted again. 'Are you a reader of the *roman-policier*, Monsieur?'

His sarcasm cut like acid. 'I *was* a detective,' Raven said stiffly.

Suzini took a second look at Raven's passport. It was new and bore no reference to his former occupation. Suzini returned the document to Raven.

'You are staying with Mademoiselle Macfarlane?'

'We live together,' Kirstie said coolly.

Suzini ignored her, concentrating on Raven. 'I want to

31

make certain things clear to you, Monsieur. This is Paris – a city under constant assault by malefactors. Even as we talk, serious crimes are being committed. Murder, rape, armed robbery. The *police-judiciare* is hard-pressed enough without having its time wasted and its resources taxed by foreigners without a sense of civic duty. Do I make myself clear, Monsieur?'

'Very clear.' A flush crept from Raven's neck to his face. The knowledge thickened his tongue. 'You're being insulting and aggressive, Monsieur. Let me remind you that I'm reporting a crime, not committing one.'

Suzini mopped his forehead with a dirty handkerchief, looking at them both with open hostility.

'You walk in here with a cock-and-bull story about some burglary where nothing was stolen, a burglary you don't report for two days. Then you complain of an assault, horseplay with other foreigners. On top of that you are offensive with my officers. My advice to you, Monsieur, is to tread very delicately. Do you understand?'

Raven looked him full in the eye. 'Yes. I understand.' He took Kirstie by the arm, speaking in English. 'Let's get the hell out of here!'

He hurried her past the sentry on the steps outside and went twenty yards before exploding. 'The bastard!'

They waited for the signals to change so that they could cross the street. Then he rushed her to the opposite pavement.

'I hope you've learned your lesson,' she gasped.

'I can't be taught what I already know,' he said obstinately.

She glanced back at the police-station. 'I wish we'd never gone near the place.'

He dropped the self-addressed envelope in the corner post-box. 'You don't think that I'll let it go at that, do you?'

Her hair swung as she shook her head. Her scarf was in her hand. 'Never in a million years. Inspector Raven has an image to sustain.'

THREE

THE NARROW STREET dropped precipitously, the shabby
buildings on each side seeming to lean in towards one another
over the speeding car. Glancing up at the rear-view mirror,
De Wayne could just about see Raven picking himself up
in a flurry of pigeons. *John Raven*. The name had been on
the guy's credit cards. De Wayne reached over and switched
off the radio.

'Take it easy,' he said quietly, his eyes resting on Tyler.
There was something suspect about Tyler's bravado. It had
shown on the previous night when he'd waited outside in
the car while De Wayne followed the elderly couple into the
apartment-building. He'd hung around until the elevator
began its ascent before starting his climb. Cracks of light
showed on some of the landings but the top floor was in utter
darkness. There was no sound at all from inside the flat.
He'd put the pencil-flash in his mouth, holding it in his
teeth to leave both hands free, the way he'd seen it done in
the movies. He'd also seen the way they sprang locks with a
piece of celluloid but the manoeuvre was more difficult in
practice. It had taken him twenty minutes moving the pliable
strip in the interstice between the door and the jamb.
Suddenly the piece of celluloid was bending back on itself
in the lock-casing. A gentle push with his shoulder and he
was in the darkened hallway. He followed the slender beam
of light through the open door and into the sleeping girl's
bedroom.

33

He held his breath, tiptoeing forward, the gun in his pocket making a reassuring weight. The girl lay with her mouth open, a fan of blonde hair over her eyes, unmoving as he searched first the clothes-closet and then her purse. The guest-room next door was unused. There were no clothes there, no personal belongings and the closets were empty. He climbed the iron circular staircase to the big room above. His luck was no better there. He looked through the desk and the drawers, rummaged through photographic equipment, opened thirty-five-millimetre cameras. It took him some time to go through the many boxes of negatives. There was no sign of what he wanted. It was physically possible for the girl to have developed the rolls of film but she had no dark-room. The negatives had to be somewhere else.

He straightened his back and looked around. He had left no sign of his visit as far as he could detect. He snapped off his flashlight and crept down the circular staircase, stopped in the hall and listened. He could hear no sound from the girl's bedroom. He opened the front door and let himself out very quietly.

The street was empty. He dropped the piece of celluloid in the river and climbed back into the car. Tyler's outburst took him completely by surprise.

'What do you mean, you couldn't find them?' Tyler's voice was shaking. 'Then what the fuck kept you? There's a fortune at stake and we're behaving like a couple of small-time hoodlums!'

De Wayne grabbed the other man's sleeve and shook his arm. 'Don't talk to me like that, Kent!' His voice had a cutting edge. 'Don't ever do it again!'

Tyler brushed his hand across his mouth. 'I'm sorry. But you don't know what it's like, goddammit, sitting here, waiting. Your blood running cold every time someone opens a door. You're sure that the film wasn't in the apartment?'

'I'm sure,' said De Wayne.

They drove back to the hunting-lodge under cover of darkness. The station-wagon was expendable now. Tyler called the garage in Sully-la-Forêt first thing the following morning, using one of the Milan false identities. A driver from the car-hire firm delivered the Peugeot shortly after nine o'clock. Tyler and De Wayne had given the youth a lift back to town on their way to Paris. They kept the house on Quai d'Anjou under surveillance for the rest of the day.

Tyler's gloved hands spun the steering-wheel. The car was too small for his comfort, forcing him to sit awkwardly. Both windows were down but his upper lip was beaded with sweat.

'We'll have to get these plates off fast,' he said, looking sideways at De Wayne. 'That bastard will have taken the numbers.'

'Relax,' said De Wayne and pointed. 'Over there where it says PARKING.'

Tyler turned the Peugeot into the car park well out of range of the checker sitting at the barrier. De Wayne slipped out of the car and unfastened the licence plates, using a coin as a screwdriver. He dropped both plates down a storm-grating, replaced the originals and took his place, wiping his hands.

'Now you see us, now you don't.'

Tyler ignored the sally, sour-faced. They crossed the river and parked in a small square opposite the Bibliothèque Nationale. They were two miles at least from the Ile St Louis and well off the tourist track. They walked across to the *Fleur-de-Lys Café* and sat down at an outside table. They had discarded their gloves but both men were still wearing sunglasses. De Wayne ordered coffee and bought a copy of the *Herald-Tribune* from a coloured girl in beach-shorts. The coffee was even worse than usual.

'We're making too many goddam mistakes,' Tyler said heavily. He had a habit of slightly squaring his shoulders whenever a statement was arguable.

De Wayne wriggled, his eye on the coloured student. 'He must have pulled a switch on us. I tell you, the guy had the stuff in his hand. I saw it. I was standing right next to him.'

Tyler sipped the water that had accompanied the coffee, his face moody. 'Well, you can bet that the police have it by now.'

De Wayne dragged his eyes away from the girl's firm round bottom. 'That's been on the cards ever since yesterday. So what? Look at it the worst way. The guy takes those rolls of film to the fuzz and tells his story. The police check the numbers of the station-wagon. What happens then?'

Tyler gave it a moment's thought. 'The computer at *Landspolizei* HQ throws out a card that says Kent Tyler, Karl Muellerstrasse, United States citizen and European Director of Didrixon & Loeb.'

De Wayne nodded quickly. 'That's right. A man of impeccable background who happens to be on holiday. OK, next question. They check out the tags on the Peugeot and find they belong to another vehicle. Where does that put them? I mean, come on now, Kent! Nothing's really *happened*, for crissakes. No one got killed. Nothing was stolen.'

'That guy's going to holler his head off.'

'Raven? He's an asshole. They'll throw him out of the office.'

'I'm not so sure.' Tyler dragged cigarette-smoke deep into his lungs. 'I don't want the Düsseldorf cops asking questions.'

'Asking questions?' De Wayne tapped his finger on the table and pointed it at Tyler. 'You're a cop, right? And someone comes in with a story like that. What do you do? The girl types it and you file it in the trash basket. It's too outrageous.'

The tension seemed to leave Tyler's frame and he stretched his legs. 'I guess you're right. This thing's beginning to get to me. But we can't afford any more mistakes.'

'There won't be any,' De Wayne said with assurance. 'Another two days and we're out of the country.'

Tyler removed his sunglasses and wiped the corners of his eyes. He was about to say something, changed his mind and called the waiter. He ordered a couple of Ricards. De Wayne sniffed the cloudy drink. It always reminded him of mouthwash. Neither he nor Tyler had completed the police-forms as required by the *Contrôle des Etrangers*. The hunting-lodge had been rented through a firm of real-estate agents in the name of an English writer who needed solitude. De Wayne's bond with Tyler went back nine years to a night aboard the United States troopship *General W. O. Darby*, six hundred miles out in the South China Sea. The poker game in the mess-room had been going for sixteen hours when De Wayne decided to quit, fourteen hundred dollars ahead. A gung-ho major had taken exception to De Wayne's withdrawal and a quarrel had broken out. The major cold-cocked De Wayne and went aloft to take the air. The only person to see De Wayne follow the major up on deck was Tyler, who reached the top of the companionway in time to see the major disappearing into the dark wet night, feet uppermost. De Wayne had been standing with his back to a ventilator. They'd stared at one another for fully a minute, then both had gone below. Tyler had never opened his mouth to anyone about what he'd seen. A thorough search of the ship followed General Assembly and the major was posted as MISSING AT SEA.

Tyler spoke suddenly. 'Scotti worries me. What the fuck's he doing in there with the door locked all the while?'

De Wayne waved elegantly. 'Professional secrets. He doesn't want us to see what goes on. Don't be a yoyo, Kent. I came to Scotti with the right introductions but he still takes us for a couple of dipsticks. *Amachoors!* He doesn't have the first idea what's happening.'

Tyler grunted. 'I don't like secrets.'

De Wayne put his head on one side. 'Talking about secrets, I've been asking myself all these years why you never turned me in that night.'

Tyler put his heel on his cigarette-stub. 'I've asked myself the same question. Maybe I was scared.'

De Wayne's dark eyes were very bright. 'I thought of that too. One thing's for certain. I'm the monkey on your back and vice versa. It's just as well we happen to trust one another.'

Tyler showed his teeth and looked at his wrist-watch. The street-lamps had been on for some time. 'Almost eight o'clock. We might as well eat before we go back.'

'You eat,' said De Wayne. 'I'm not hungry. Besides, there's something I want to do.'

'Like what?' Tyler dropped his sunglasses in his pocket. De Wayne followed suit. 'I have to see someone.'

Their eyes locked across the table and Tyler was first to break off. 'Well, be back by ten. I'll be dining across the square.'

De Wayne walked away without looking back. A cab took him to Neuilly. The condominium was an eight-storey building with no architectural pretensions. Lights blazed on all floors. The swimming-pool and plane-trees in the front were floodlit. Illuminated box-signs showed the way in and out of the underground garage. De Wayne used his key, letting himself into a lobby with gilt chairs and a red carpet. The apartment was on his left, a white door with an optic-glass spyhole and a Jewish scroll attached to the lintel. He unlocked the door and stepped into a hallway decorated with flocked wallpaper. He pushed the door shut and stood there listening to the sound of Duke Ellington coming from the bedroom. A woman appeared in the doorway. Her Slav inheritance showed in her wide-set eyes and cheekbones. Straw-coloured hair was chopped in a *gamine* cut. She wore a silk shirt with velvet pants that made the most of her figure. Her fine-skinned face was slashed with lines. She could have been the thirty she appeared but was five years older. Iceberg eyes questioned him, then she came towards him quickly.

'What happened? What's the matter?'

He put his mouth on hers and shook his head. 'We blew it this evening with the guy, Fran. Kent's having a helluva time convincing himself that it doesn't matter.'

She went into the bedroom and silenced the music. Then she joined him in the long sitting-room. He poured himself a glass of rye and explained what had happened. She knelt on the bearskin rug listening. The flat was ostentatiously vulgar with suede-upholstered furniture and garish abstract paintings. The owner was an Alsatian banker familiarly known as Sig the Sod. His wife had worked with Fran in a couple of Broadway musicals. The Hochheims were in Tobago and had lent Fran the apartment. She glanced up when De Wayne had finished.

'How bad is it, honey?' Her voice was quiet.

They had lived together for four years, surviving in places where they had no right to be. Places like Vegas and Acapulco. A twister had flattened the walls of the Barn Theatre, ending De Wayne's dream of an Ionesco season, and in Mexico Fran's act folded after ten days of a three-month engagement. He had seen her show anger and alarm but he had never seen her running scared.

'We're all right,' he said, and replenished his glass. The gilt candlesticks had come from a synagogue in Czestochowa and the kitsch cigarette-box was from London's Portobello Road. He added dry ginger to the whisky. Fran rarely drank or smoked and, though she'd taken the odd joint at a party, she'd never been known to buy the stuff.

'It isn't blowing it that bothers me,' he said, looking down where she sprawled on the rug. 'It's the way Kent's acting.'

She lit a cigarette, holding the match with sun-tanned fingers. 'Do you think that he knows about us?'

He blew smoke and considered the suggestion. 'I guess so,' he said finally. 'I mean, I think that he guesses. I've never even mentioned your name, let alone the fact that you're here in Paris. But Kent's no dummy. What he certainly doesn't know is that we're splitting just as soon as he cashes in.'

She went on combing through the bearskin rug with her fingernails. She suddenly looked up at him, grimacing.

'Costa Rica! My God! Bad gin, scorpions and chicks trying to make like Rita Moreno.'

He shrugged. 'Kent won't mind as long as he thinks he'll have company. He has a different way of looking at things.

The way he sees it is that absolute safety in a banana jungle is better than treading delicately in luxury.'

She laughed, came to her feet and ruffled his hair fondly. 'You're wicked and that's why I love you. When do you think that we'll move?'

He had siphoned off a couple of thousand dollars from his expense money and used it to buy the convertible in the underground car-park, a chance buy from the FOR SALE columns in the Paris edition of the *Herald-Tribune*. Three years old with forty thousand miles on the clock, a recent overhaul and new tyres. He bought it in Fran's name. The plan was for her to drive it to Zürich and wait for him there. He and Tyler were going straight to a chalet in the mountains outside Zürich. The shareout was due to take place there. Like the rest of the scheme, this had been agreed from the start. Once they'd divided their haul, each man was supposed to find his own way to Costa Rica via Mexico City.

'It all depends when Scotti finishes the run. He's another headache but as least he can be handled. In any case, there's no sense in you hanging around in Zürich waiting for me. As soon as I know, I'll call you. And while I think of it . . .' He held out his hand.

She took the two apartment keys. 'I'll fix something to eat,' he said. She beat him to the kitchen with its control panel and battery of electronic devices. The only food in the refrigerator was some smoked salmon, curling at the edges. 'Jesus,' he said, sighing. He grinned before she could take offence. 'Don't worry, honey. That'll be fine!'

He watched her cut the slices of lemon and bread, the peel still on the lemon. Fran had her talents but housekeeping wasn't one of them. He ate the sandwich standing with his back against the refrigerator. It was a quarter past nine.

'I'll call you the moment Kent gives the word,' he promised, wiping his mouth. 'You know what to do.'

She nodded. He put the plate down and drew a rough map showing the mountain chalet in relation to the hotel where she would be staying.

'This is where we'll be,' he said, pointing. 'It's on the

40

south side of the lake about fourteen miles out of town. I don't want you to move from that hotel. Sit on the phone. I'll need you to come and pick me up.'

She moved with a dancer's grace to take his face between her palms. 'Trust me?' she asked.

'Sure,' he nodded. 'This is another world, Fran. A whole new ball game.'

'I know it,' she said and smiled. 'When you need me, whistle.'

A cab let him off on Square Louvois.

The *Richelieu* was a small, expensive and discreetly run hotel. Tyler was waiting in the foyer, smoking a cigar over his coffee. He came to his feet, seeing De Wayne.

'The bill's paid. Let's go.'

They crossed the square to the rented Peugeot. Tyler was a night-blind driver and De Wayne took the wheel. Tyler buckled his seat-belt.

'Was everything all right?'

The motor caught. De Wayne glanced up in the rear-view mirror and went into low gear. He made his voice casual.

'Sure.'

'That's good,' Tyler said pleasantly. De Wayne turned his head but his partner's face was innocent.

It was after ten when they drove out of Paris. Twenty miles south of the city rain started pattering on the roof. Another fifteen miles took them deep into the forest, forty-two thousand acres of beech, birch and oak. The wet road unreeled in front of the flicking windscreen wipers. Head-lamps pierced thick glades, rocky wildernesses and sandy clearings. Once in the town of Fontainebleau, they waited for the signals to change. Elegant streets were forlorn under dripping trees. Café lights shone across glistening pavements. The bunting stretched across the streets was sodden and what few pedestrians there were hurried past beneath umbrellas. Bourgeois villas were shuttered against the misery outside.

De Wayne jerked his head towards two policemen sheltering in a bank doorway.

'I wouldn't have thought there'd be much need for the
law in a town like this. You can bet even the whores pay
taxes and go to church.'

Tyler smiled thinly. His choice of the area had come after
much study of the atlas. Sully-la-Forêt was only sixty-nine
kilometres from Paris and within easy reach of Switzerland.

The signals changed and De Wayne swung the Peugeot
into the green-lit lane. The sheltering cops watched indiffer-
ently. Eight miles west of Fontainebleau, Sully-la-Forêt
showed as a diffused glow in the rain ahead. The small town
looked deserted, the shops along the main avenue closed and
shuttered. The lights they had seen came from the hotel
and *gendarmerie*. De Wayne turned on to a road that led
straight back into the forest. A couple of miles out of town
it narrowed. The area was popular among wealthy Parisians.
Their weekend villas were ringed with fences and spiked
with cautionary notices. Bridlepaths meandered through
the dripping trees. The only sound was of rain rattling on the
roof and the squelch of the tyres.

They forded a stream and turned a bend in the road. A
signpost read PAVILLON SARRAULT. Iron gates set in a tall
brick wall opened on to a drive in bad repair. The
Peugeot jolted over a cattle-grid. Massive oaks appeared
through the downpour. The hunting-lodge was long and low
and built of yellow stone. The stables had been converted
to a four-car garage with staff quarters above. De Wayne
eased the car in beside the station-wagon and Tyler dropped
the cantilever doors. They stood in the darkness, the rain
falling steadily outside. Tyler opened the door to the vast
stoneflagged kitchen. Meathooks hung in the blackened
chimney-piece, a carved wooden crucifix on a whitewashed
wall.

Only the refrigerator and freezer were modern. The
table and chairs might well have come from the stables. The
cooking-stove ran on bottled gas. The remains of the Italian's

supper were on the draining-board. Tyler's lips came together.

'Why the fuck can't he wash-up like the rest of us?'

He tipped bread and sausage skins into the rubbish bin. Music was playing somewhere. They walked along the corridor to the billiard-room. No lights showed and the door was locked. It had taken their joint efforts to manhandle the printing-press up on to the billiard-table. The slate bed made a perfect base for it. They'd piled mattresses and pillows against the window-embrasures. The nearest neighbours were six kilometres away. De Wayne and Tyler bought the food in Paris. Neither man had shown himself in the town. Except for the youth who had delivered the Peugeot, nobody had come near the lodge since they had been there.

Tyler's look was questioning. De Wayne hunched his shoulders. 'Your guess is as good as mine. Maybe he's gone to bed.'

They followed the sound of the music down the corridor, past portraits of Sarrault cavaliers in plumed hats, patched and powdered ladies fondling pop-eyed dogs. Scotti was in the library, flat on his back on the floor, his teeth clenched on a Tuscan cheroot. His shoes were off and he was still wearing his gloves. As far as De Wayne could tell, he wore them in his sleep. He was listening to Tyler's transistor. Scotti removed the cheroot from his mouth and looked up, grinning.

Tyler's voice was unsteady. 'I told you to keep that goddam door locked. We could have had the entire police-force all over the house and you wouldn't have known the difference.'

'Bullshit,' said Scotti. His overalls were splashed with printer's ink. He put the cheroot back in his mouth and blew smoke deliberately. 'I heard you a couple of miles away. So I opened the door. Whatsamatter, you guys, anyway?'

De Wayne stepped in to break it up. 'It's been a long day. How did the work go?'

Scotti hoisted himself to his feet and trod back into his

shoes. 'Beautiful! But what you expect? I'm a best in a fucking business.'

He started back towards the billiard-room. They heard the door being opened noisily, the Italian whistling. Tyler silenced the radio. 'That prick keeps the key in his pocket,' he said bitterly.

De Wayne shrugged. 'So what? If it keeps him happy.'

Scotti was back, carrying an armful of finished bonds. He selected one from the middle of the pile and tossed it down on the table. Tyler took it to the lamp. De Wayne looked over his shoulder. Colour, design and texture, all were perfect. The serial numbers were in perfect alignment and identical with those used in the genuine issue.

Scotti showed unlovely teeth, obviously pleased with himself. He moved closer to Tyler and De Wayne.

'Tomorrow night we finish.'

His breath stank and Tyler averted his head fastidiously. 'They're good,' he said grudgingly.

'Damn right, they're good,' said Scotti. 'You ain't gonna see no better. I stay here another week you could take over that fucking corporation.'

De Wayne clapped him on the back. 'You're a genius, that's what.'

Scotti grunted, his eyes cunning as he looked from one to the other. 'You mugs don't know from nothing,' he said contemptuously. Then he yawned and stretched. 'I'm gonna take a bath and hit the sack.' He left the room, taking Tyler's radio with him.

'That wop's beginning to get to me,' Tyler said at the door.

De Wayne poured himself a glass of whisky. 'I noticed.' He raised the glass. 'To all those things we never had and are just about to get!'

Tyler nodded, unsmiling. Sound of water running came from upstairs. He turned the key in the lock. Then he swung back a section of bookcase, revealing what looked like a meat-safe. A fifteen-year-old with time to spare and a power-drill could have removed the old-fashioned handle. The

44

heavy door swung outwards under Tyler's pressure. He placed the bearer-bonds on the top shelf. De Wayne could smell the sickly sweet odour of the plastic explosive on the second shelf. Explosive and detonators had come from a United States Army establishment in Kaiserlautern. On the bottom shelf were the false passports and papers he had bought in Milan, together with embossing stamps for whatever photographs were used. Tyler closed the safe and swung back the section of bookcase. He put a match to the driving-licence he had used to hire the Peugeot and watched it burn in the fireplace. He checked his watch and turned on the television on the table. The image built quickly, the announcer's voice quick and assured. The newcast was short. There was no mention of an assault on a foreigner in Paris. Tyler switched off the set.

De Wayne looked at him, grinning, balancing the glass of scotch on his knee. 'What did you expect, Batman?'

The sally went unappreciated. Tyler poured himself a shot from the whisky bottle and sat down heavily, his face in shadow. The house had been unoccupied since the previous autumn and the chill touch of winter was still in its fabric.

'I'm tired,' Tyler said suddenly. 'Know what I mean? Tired of looking over my shoulder for some smart prick waiting to trip me up. I'm tired and I'm lonely.'

De Wayne emptied his glass. 'You've lost your kid. It's bound to have left a hole in your life.'

Tyler moved his head from side to side, his face still out of focus. 'Ah, she was always her mother's child. It isn't that. How about you, Rod?'

'How about me what?'

'Don't you ever get lonely?'

De Wayne's sun-tanned face was reflective. 'I'm not the lonely kind,' he said at last. 'People come and go. I've always thought a lot about what happens when you get old. If nobody loves you by then you'd better be rich. That way when you bang your cane on the floor they'll still come running. I

45

never really thought I was lovable. Come to think of it, nor are you.'

Tyler's cropped white head lifted. 'No, not even on a good day. But you've got that all under control, haven't you?'

'You mean Fran?' It was the first time Tyler had referred to her.

Tyler's teeth showed in a humourless smile. 'Whatever her name is. The lady you go to see. The one who called you when we were in the motel in Kreefeld. Is she coming to Costa Rica?'

The water had stopped running up in the bathroom. The sound of the rain on the window-panes disturbed the sudden silence. De Wayne shook his head.

'Don't you know me better than that, Kent?'

Tyler put his glass down very carefully. 'Who the hell knows you? People may think that they do.'

'She's not coming to Costa Rica,' said De Wayne.

'Why not? Don't you trust her? She's come this far with you.' There was an acidity in Tyler's voice that made the words more than just banter.

'There's no question of trust,' lied De Wayne. 'You've got it all wrong. Fran takes whatever comes her way and she doesn't ask questions. It's what you call a perfect understanding. She also knows that this is the end of the line.'

'I'm delighted to hear it. I mean, there are secrets that you and I share that can't be shared with anyone else. Know what I mean, Rod?'

De Wayne cleared his throat. 'No, I don't know what you mean.'

Tyler offered his bleak smile again. 'You threw Bill Kerkorian overboard.'

The accusation created a picture. The *General W. O. Darby* wallowing in the South China Sea, a body flashing down into the wet darkness.

'You've waited a long time to say that,' said De Wayne. 'Sure, I put the bastard over the side but you already knew that.' The image held, spray blowing on the wind, the lonely stretch of deck and, at the top of the companionway, Tyler's face caught in the light from the salt-encrusted lamp. It was a younger face and the hair was black instead of white but the look then was the same as now.

'I wanted to be sure,' said Tyler. The gilt clock chimed melodiously above the fireplace. 'What I never understood was why you weren't investigated.'

'What makes you think that I wasn't?' De Wayne asked. 'You left ship in Honolulu, remember. They put me under arrest four hours out of San Diego. The moment we were back in Fort Ord, Criminal Investigation Command was all over me. Everyone except you in that poker-game made a statement. A couple of them claimed to have seen me follow Kerkorian up on deck. But the only evidence they had was circumstantial. They finally gave me the lie-detector test.'

'And?' Tyler's face was frankly curious.

De Wayne's hands lifted. 'I thought positive.'

'How come you never mentioned this before?' said Tyler.

De Wayne followed the other man to his feet. 'You never asked me.'

They extinguished the lights and climbed the stairs. The corridor ran the length of the hunting-lodge. There were three bedrooms and a bathroom on either side. Linen-closets were set beneath the windows at the ends of the corridor. The servants' quarters were reached by back stairs from the kitchen. De Wayne drew his curtains and put on pyjamas and robe. He padded down to the bathroom, his bare feet noiseless on the carpet. Scotti had left his wet towels on the floor and the tub was filthy. De Wayne scrubbed it and found clean towels. Tyler had been strange tonight, almost menacing. De Wayne lay in the pine-scented water and thought about it. But when he left the bath he was no further ahead. He dried himself, brushed his teeth and turned off the wall-heater. There were no lights showing in the corridor. He put an ear to the Italian's door and heard the rasping breathing. He tried the handle gently. The door was locked on

the other side. He moved across towards his own room.
Tyler's voice came from the darkness.

'Goodnight, Rod.'

'Goodnight,' said De Wayne and closed his door. For
some odd reason his heart was beating much faster than
usual.

FOUR

THE CURTAINS WERE OPEN and the rain had stopped. Tyler shut his eyes and went over his plan yet again. The Range Rover was hidden half a mile away, under a tarpaulin. He had bought the vehicle at an auction in England, registered and insured it in a false name and driven to France. The Range Rover had been in the forest for the last five weeks. He heard a noise and opened his eyes, half-expecting to see someone standing in the doorway. But the sound was only part of the house settling down for the night. Metal creaked. Pipes rumbled. Feet scurried over the loft above. Outside in the forest, life and death continued their dance, stalker and quarry moving inexorably. He raised himself on an elbow, feeling for the glass of water. He swallowed a couple of Mogadon tablets and composed himself to sleep. The face of the small clock glowed in the darkness, the hands folded at midnight.

The next time he looked at the clock it was seven o'clock in the morning. He shaved and put on his blue flannel suit, then went downstairs to the kitchen. His face was calm in the kitchen mirror. It was ten minutes before De Wayne appeared, elegant in houndstooth checks and a cashmere sweater. De Wayne poured himself a cup of coffee, wrinkling his nose at the burnt toast.

'Make fresh,' said Tyler. 'How did you sleep?'

'Well,' said De Wayne from the mirror. 'Like an honest man.' He fed bread into the toaster, glancing out into the cobbled courtyard. Sunshine was streaming in across the

49

stone-flagged kitchen. De Wayne carried his coffee and
toast to the table. Scotti appeared at eight o'clock, wet hair
slicked over his pallid scalp and wearing his ink-spattered
overalls. His eyes looked as though they had never closed
in his life. He sliced into his coarse garlic sausage and
clamped the slices between pieces of bread. He ate and drank
noisily, grabbing at the pit of his stomach and belching.

'I'm working right through today. One of you guys can
bring me my lunch. We ought to be finished around seven.'

'You said six last night.' Tyler tried not to make much of
it but his schedule depended on accuracy.

Scotti spat sausage-skin on to the floor. 'We're not running
no railroad here. It depends.'

De Wayne looked across from the shaft of sunlight.
'Depends on what?'

Scotti was in no hurry to answer. He cut through one of
his twisted cheroots with the bread knife and stuck half in
his mouth.

'The power's not regular, know what I mean? It comes
and goes. I got to watch the colour-control all the time.'

Neither of the other men spoke. Scotti took his plate and
cup to the sink, turned and shook his head at Tyler.

'Whatsamatter with you, anyway?'

Tyler wet his lips, choosing his words with the delicacy
of a diamond sorter.

'I'm sorry, I don't understand you.'

'I'm sorry, I don't understand you!' The Italian's voice
was a parody of Tyler's. Scotti made a fist and jerked his
arm. 'You've had a hard on for me ever since I got here. No
respect. Who the fuck you guys think you are?'

De Wayne moved between them easily. 'We love you,
maestro. You're the best thing that ever happened to us.'
His smile was wide and warm.

The Italian made a sound of disgust, blowing a cloud of
tobacco-smoke in Tyler's direction.

'What chance have I got here – a creep and a bullshit
artist! Well, just don't forget I got a deadline too. I want
to be out of this dump eight o'clock latest.'

'We won't forget,' Tyler said quietly. The Italian's flight left Charles de Gaulle at five minutes to midnight.

Scotti grinned like a pawnbroker asked for charity. A couple of minutes later the printing-press started up, reverberating in the timbers and sending the utensils dancing on the kitchen dresser. De Wayne clipped the table with his buttocks. He was still standing in the sunshine, polishing the tip of a Gucci loafer against the back of his trouser leg.

'What do you want me to do? I'm already packed.'

Neither of them had bothered about leaving fingerprints though the army had both sets on record. Tyler had never deluded himself. It was simply a matter of time before the bonds were found to be forgeries and his own role established. But by then he would be in Costa Rica.

'Check the rooms,' he said. 'His as well. Make sure that nothing's left lying around.'

'You got it.' De Wayne pushed up off the table. 'Nothing to remember us by.' He winked, sun-tanned and feisty, the guy you always wanted on your side. He opened the door to the corridor. The sound of the press was louder.

Tyler climbed the stairs to the servants' quarters. The room had an iron bed covered with thin blankets. A cheap Moroccan rug lay on the floor. Plastic flowers bloomed in a vase. Someone had forgotten a string of rosary beads. He pulled a chair to the window and panned the binoculars across the grass and sunken garden to the entrance-gates and approach road. The forest was green and fresh, the earth steaming in the morning sunshine. Off to the right, a change of colour indicated where the Range Rover was hidden. Tyres and battery were new, the fuel tank full. A sturdy four-wheel drive would take the vehicle through any hazard that the forest might offer.

Movement caught his eye. He panned quickly, refocusing. The image grew clearer. A rider was cantering his horse along the grass verge towards the entrance-gates. Tyler dropped the binoculars, tore downstairs and hammered on the billiard-room door. A couple of valuable minutes passed before it was opened. Scotti had a sun-visor pulled low on his forehead. His shirtsleeves were pulled up to his elbows, his gloves soaked in ink. Smoke filled the shuttered room. Tyler yanked the power-plug from the wall. The press stopped abruptly.

'Somebody's coming,' he said. 'Keep out of sight.'

The door closed quickly. He raced for the stairs. The thirty-eight was up in his bedroom. He found the weapon and stuffed it into his jacket pocket. He looked up to find De Wayne standing in the doorway. The house was strangely quiet.

'A guy on a horse,' said Tyler, pushing past. 'He's coming this way.' They sprinted down to the library window.

The man had dismounted and was trying to haul the reluctant chestnut by the reins across the cattle-grid. De Wayne's face was tense. 'What happens now?'

Tyler motioned him away from the window. 'We get rid of him.'

De Wayne glanced down at the gun in Tyler's hand. 'You're out of your mind!'

'For crissakes,' Tyler said impatiently. He stuffed the revolver back in his pocket and looked through the window again. The man was back in the saddle, the horse over the grid. Tyler jerked his head towards the corridor.

'Go out the back. Work your way round and see where he goes.'

They both ran from the room, De Wayne towards the kitchen, Tyler to the front door. The heavy key worked stiffly. He wrenched the bolts back, his mouth suddenly dry.

The rider trotted up the driveway, posting, looking around him curiously. He dismounted, chucked the reins over the horse's head and walked towards Tyler. He was a florid man in a yellow waistcoat and a hacking-jacket. His riding-boots had the sheen of fresh tar.

'*Bonjour, Monsieur*,' he said, nodding at Tyler. '*Madame Sarrault est chez elle?*'

Tyler moved his head from side to side, speaking in English. 'I'm sorry, I don't understand French.'

'*Gilles Tennier*,' said the Frenchman, enunciating very

clearly. *'Je cherche Madame de Sarrault.'*

'Not here,' said Tyler. 'Partee!'

'Madame n'est pas là?' Tennier's voice was uncertain.

'Pah eecee,' answered Tyler. 'Safari in Kenya.' He fired an imaginary rifle. 'Afreek!'

Tennier's face cleared as he found the clue he needed. *'Ah bon! Madame fait la chasse! Je m'excuse, Monsieur.'* He put his foot in the stirrup. Their smiles held as he tried to mount. The chestnut backed off, ears flattened. Tyler held the horse's head until the Frenchman was safely in the saddle. Tennier lifted a hand.

'Au revoir, Monsieur, et merci!' He cantered off down the driveway.

Tyler shut the front door and leaned his forehead against the cool paintwork. Sweat had sprung in his hair and ran cold on his flanks. The hollow strike of the horse's hoofs grew fainter. He had a feeling of emptiness in his stomach as if he hadn't eaten for days. He went to the library window. Tennier had negotiated the cattle-grid and was trotting down the grass verge beyond. It was five minutes before De Wayne appeared in the kitchen. His loafers were stained with water, his elegant trousers thorn-snagged. He ran a glass of water and gulped it. He wiped his mouth on the back of his hand.

'Which way did he go?' asked Tyler.

De Wayne pointed in the direction of the oak-trees. 'He didn't look in any hurry. What do you think?'

Tyler's confidence was rebuilding. 'Some friend of the woman who owns the place. I guess he didn't know that she'd rented.'

De Wayne was wiping his shoes with a towel. 'He must have heard that goddam press.'

Tyler shrugged. 'So what? There's no way that he could have known what it was. In any case, the noise could have been coming from the woods.'

They walked along the corridor to the billiard-room. Scotti opened to Tyler's knocking. His eyes flicked from one to the other.

'A false alarm,' said Tyler. 'A guy with the wrong address.'

Scotti's scowl lighted on De Wayne. 'I shoulda run the moment I put eyes on you. I need my head examined.'

The printing-press behind him glinted under the green-shaded light, its control panel mysterious. The finished bonds were neatly stacked on the billiard-table, each one crisp and convincing, a promise of five thousand dollars. Scotti stuck the power-plug back in the wall and jerked his head, herding them out of the room.

'Get outa here and leave me be,' he said, and slammed the door in their faces. The press started up immediately.

'A really nice guy,' said Tyler. 'It'll be a pleasure to see the back of him.'

It was difficult to hear with the noise of the press. De Wayne walked him back as far as the kitchen. They stopped outside the door.

'Take it easy,' De Wayne said quietly. 'There's a long way to go.'

Tyler recognised the faint note of contempt. His wife's voice sounded again in his head. *A little man in a big body. That's what you are, Kent Tyler. A fake!*

'Sure,' he said, smiling. 'I'll take it easy.'

He resumed his post at the window, watching the approach road and forest. Squirrels were grubbing for food under the oak-trees. His mind went to Zürich. He'd incorporated Chase Mutual six months before in the State of Delaware. Its charter allowed the company to deal in stocks and securities. He'd rented premises in Zürich and hired a Swiss secretary who was bilingual. She knew him as Peterson. He used the same name when opening the bank account for Chase Mutual. The girl had spent the last month typing out Tyler's old market analyses. His next appearance in the city was in his role as Düsseldorf Director of Didrixon & Loeb. He informed the bank in confidence of a new corporate policy. Didrixon & Loeb were about to invest in the bearer-bond market and were interested in the General Chemical issues. The bank officer had approved his choice and assured him of their readiness to advance up to ninety per cent of the market value of bonds lodged with the bank as collateral. Tyler was going to pay the charges on the loan for a year, ensuring that the bonds would stay buried in the vaults at least for that period. There was no way in which his scheme could misfire as long as he kept his cool. Handelskredit knew him as Didrixon & Loeb's trusted executive.

He yawned nervously, thinking about the hours ahead. Experts had trained him in the martial arts. He had learned how to kill with flame, weapons and bare hands. All of these skills had been put to use in Vietnam. The need to survive had powered him then. It would power him now. He went to the top of the stairs and called down. De Wayne strolled along the corridor, holding his place in the book he was reading. He looked like a man in his club, called to the telephone. Tyler was never quite sure which was the man and which the actor.

'Take over,' he said. 'I'll fix the food.'

De Wayne showed his thumb and went upstairs. Tyler put potatoes on the stove, washed spinach and rubbed pepper on the steaks. This was going to be the last meal the three of them had together. He carried the Italian's tray to the billiard-room and tapped on the door. It was close in the shuttered room, the air vitiated and thick with tobacco-smoke. The Italian was sweating but showed no signs of suffering. He took the tray and kicked the door shut. Tyler climbed the back stairs with the second tray. He put it on the bed.

'*Guten appetit!*'

De Wayne lifted his feet from the blankets. His loafers were stained but dry. He took a plate and a glass of red wine from the tray.

'I've been watching the crows,' he said, jerking his head at the scene outside. 'Aren't those mothers something! They know all the angles.'

Tyler dragged another chair to the window. 'I grew up in the country,' he said shortly.

De Wayne cocked his head and turned the corners of

his mouth down. 'Is that right?' He shifted his fork from his left hand to his right and speared a piece of meat.

Spring sunshine flooded the grass and sunken garden. The squirrels were still busy under the trees. Tyler's voice was flat.

'I'm going to hit him just as soon as he's finished.'

De Wayne waited until his mouth was empty before he replied. 'People die all the time for one reason or another. There's no reason to get emotional.'

'I don't intend to,' said Tyler. They finished their meal in silence. Tyler collected the plates and the glasses. 'You'd better hang on here. There are a couple of things that I have to do.'

De Wayne was leaning back on a tilted chair, picking at his teeth with a broken matchstick. 'You're sure you're going to be all right?' he asked.

'Look,' said Tyler. 'The one thing I don't need is you holding my hand. This thing didn't start in some Vegas clip-joint. It started up here.' He tapped the side of his head.

He took the tray down to the kitchen and collected the fibre travelling-bag from his room. He carried it into the library and locked the door. There were two hundred and thirty bonds already in the safe. Each weighed the same as the genuine article, one point three ounces. Five hundred of them would tip the scale at just a little more than forty pounds. An easy lift. The bonds were nine inches long by six. He packed them in pouch-envelopes bearing the imprint of the Bank of America. He'd missed no trick that might help, including a HIGHLY CONFIDENTIAL letter to Südwest Verein announcing Didrixon & Loeb's acquisition of General Chemical bearer-bonds. The letter had coincided with a rise of a point in their market value.

Left in the open safe was the plastic explosive, still sweating slightly in its wrapping, the detonators and a box of shells for the thirty-eight. He took the revolver to the window. A slight haze was creeping through the gates from the forest and the squirrels had disappeared. He spun the cylinder, checking each chamber. He turned sharply, hearing someone try the door-handle. De Wayne had his mouth to the crack.

'Open up, it's me!'

Tyler moved quickly, putting the suitcase behind the sofa and closing the safe. De Wayne came into the room, looking around curiously. The light outside was beginning to fade. The sun had sunk behind the trees. A nerve was jumping under Tyler's right eye. He brushed at it uselessly. De Wayne perched on the arm of a chair, his attention drawn by the gun in Tyler's hand. De Wayne's face was bright and knowing.

'I went through his bag.'

Tyler put the gun in his jacket pocket. 'And?'

'He's hidden the ten grand in the lining.'

Tyler nodded. 'We'll get it later.' The house was suddenly quiet. The press had stopped. The two men looked at one another. Tyler's mouth was dry again. The Italian's heavy footstep sounded in the corridor. Tyler opened the door. Scotti was carrying the remainder of the bearer-bonds. He dumped them on the table.

'Mission complete! I just made you fuckers millionaires. Break out the wine.'

Tyler spoke carefully, as if playing a part newly learned. 'The wine's in the kitchen.'

The Italian checked his watch. 'One of you guys can drive me to the airport as soon as I've washed up. I'd sooner hang around there than here. This place gives me the creeps.'

'Sure,' said Tyler. He followed Scotti down the corridor towards the kitchen. He was two paces behind when he fired. The shot entered the back of Scotti's head and travelled upwards, burying itself in the Italian's brainpan. He was dead before he hit the floor. Tyler stepped over the body, his eyes and nose stinging from the acrid stink of the explosion. De Wayne was standing six feet away.

'Get a hold on his shoulders,' said Tyler. They carried Scotti's body into the billiard-room and laid it on the floor. Sightless eyes stared up at the green-shaded lamp.

De Wayne moved as Tyler fired for the second time,

swinging round with a look of disbelief. The shot took him from the front. A fountain of blood from his forehead played over his eyes, nose and mouth, staining his teeth scarlet. His mouth worked for a second like a fish out of water, then he pitched forward heavily on to his face.

Tyler cut the lights quickly and wiped the sweat from his neck. It was over, done with. No more fear. He ran to the kitchen and put his head under cold water. It took him a couple of minutes to pull himself together. It all seemed so easy now. He packed the last batch of bonds in the suitcase and left it in the hallway. He was taking nothing else. He cleared the Italian's room of clothing and changed the sheets. De Wayne's room he left as it was. The ten thousand dollars had been secreted under the lid of Scotti's bag, the lining resealed. He packed the bag with the Italian's clothing, having removed the money. He carried the bag downstairs. They'd find the remains of two bodies. De Wayne always carried his passport on him. Tyler's was upstairs in his bedroom, left with his loose cash and creditcards. Nobody knew that the Italian existed. Two bodies, two people, both easily identified.

He threw the Italian's suitcase into the billiard-room and came back holding the explosive gingerly. There was no sound or movement in the darkened room in front of him but he had to force himself to move forward and place the explosive device near the table. He wound the timing-clock and put it down gently. Then he ran. He had exactly eight minutes before the whole place went up. He drew the bolts in the hallway, the seconds ticking in his head. He jogged down the driveway in the gathering dusk, across the cattle-grid and into the shelter of the trees. He carried the bag with the bonds in both arms. He followed the stream that would take him to the hidden Range Rover. He'd gone a couple of hundred yards when a vivid flash lit the trees with sudden brilliance. The explosion that followed rumbled through the forest, shaking branches and showering torn leaves. Then the last echo died. He reached out and touched the silence.

FIVE

HE STOOD AT THE KITCHEN WINDOW, watching the pair of wood-pigeons on the roof. They left every morning to feed in some open space, returning to their roost at nightfall. It made him think of the sparrowhawk at home that patrolled the river near his houseboat. Birds and animals adapted to urban surroundings, often unnoticed. The coffee-grinder whirred behind him. Kirstie pushed her hair out of her eyes with her forearm.

'Are you hung over?'

He shook his head. He'd drunk almost half a bottle of scotch but felt none the worse for it.

'Then make yourself useful,' she said.

It was too early for croissants or bread. Madame Rambert went to the bakery at eight. He sliced a grapefruit in two and placed it on the table with a flourish. He sprinkled soft brown sugar on each half, keeping his voice casual.

'What are your plans for this morning?'

She poured the coarse-ground coffee into the percolator, her eye on the egg-timer. 'I have to pick up a skirt, otherwise nothing. Why?'

He buttered a couple of rusks with great care. 'I thought we might drive down to Fontainebleau, have some lunch there perhaps.'

She slammed two earthenware bowls on the table, one after the other, hard. 'Haven't we had enough trouble without you looking for more?'

The first bubbles were beginning to rise in the percolator.
'I can always go by myself, of course.'

She turned her head away. When the coffee was ready she filled both bowls, added cream and placed his boiled egg in front of him. She sat down opposite.

'You're a bastard at times,' she said.

He shook his head vigorously. 'Nicest chap in the business. Not just one of your ordinary ex-copper riffraff.'

Her eyes stared over the rim of her bowl, tobacco smoke blue in the sunshine.

'I refuse to believe that you're too dumb to get Suzini's message.'

He spooned the last of the egg-yolk into his mouth and pushed away the plate. He never touched the white. The scene at the Commissariat still rankled.

'I got the message all right. That's why I intend making a few inquiries on my own account.'

She put her bowl down very carefully. 'Great! Have you forgotten that you're in France. There's no Jerry Soo around the corner at the Yard to bail you out of trouble.'

'Unfair. Below the belt.' He chewed carefully, keeping the hard rusk away from his suspect filling. 'I'll have you know that I'm eminently capable of taking care of myself.'

'My God!' She raised her eyes to the ceiling dramatically. 'I shudder every time I hear that phrase. The next step is usually total disaster.'

He reached for his cigarettes. The first one of the day was always a special experience. He remained quiet as she made a production of doing the washing-up. Suddenly she swung round.

'Does it ever occur to you that we have a whole lot less to say to one another now than we did a year ago?'

Her vehemence took him totally by surprise. 'I thought we talked a lot,' he said mildly.

She put her bunched fists on her hips. 'We talk but we certainly don't *say* a lot. Most of the time it's me listening to you, in any case.' Her tone of voice was bitter.

60

'I'm sorry,' he said, looking across at her. 'I just hadn't realised. I suppose I've been my own company for too long. I'm too selfish.'

It took her some time but she smiled forgiveness. 'For a confirmed bachelor you've got some great lines, Raven. Thank God we're not married.'

'What we've got is much better,' he said, straight-faced. 'Love keeps us together.'

She burst out laughing in spite of herself. 'You're impossible.'

'Much more sensitive than you think,' he said. 'Does that mean that you'll drive me to Sully-la-Forêt?'

'Of course,' she said. She came around the table and kissed the top of his head. 'I may not give in graciously but I do give in.'

He glanced up, his arms round her waist. 'Don't worry. You win all the big ones.'

He opened the window. The wood-pigeons had gone. Early-morning workers were crossing the bridge on their way to the Métro.

'Right,' he said, stretching. 'I'll have my bath.'

He stayed in the tub for half an hour with the radio playing beside him. Then he put on his jeans and sneakers, topping a blue cotton shirt with his windbreaker. Kirstie was busy with the morning's chores. Madame Rambert had offered to help but Kirstie wouldn't have her in the apartment. A Portuguese woman came in once a week to handle the heavy work.

He took a book upstairs to the studio and sat in the sunshine, reading. It was after ten when Kirstie called up from the hallway. She was wearing her favourite colour, a pale blue linen dress with Italian sandals.

'I'm off, darling! I should be back around noon.' She blew him a kiss and then closed the door.

He waited until he heard the rattle of the elevator before leisurely following her.

He took the Métro, changing three times before he surfaced at Place de l'Opéra. He turned right on Boulevard de la Madeleine. It was April and the city was host to the best part of a million visitors. Romantics following in the footsteps of Scott Fitzgerald jostled brilliantly apparelled South Americans, Germans and Swedes. Lady-librarians were leaving a culture-tour bus. A banner over the entrance to the Scribe Hotel proclaimed a convention of Rotarians in residence. The Parisians went about their business, indifferent alike to the visitors from overseas and their own provincials. The usual band of bearded youngsters congregated in front of the American Express building, some of them lying down on the sidewalk, signs beside them requesting lifts to far-off destinations. Others were selling their return tickets home. A girl feeding a baby smiled at Raven from a parked Volkswagen with stickers from a dozen countries on the bodywork.

He made his way down to the mail-counter. A clerk glanced at his passport and found the self-addressed envelope. Raven extracted the negatives and put them in a second envelope. This he addressed to his bank in London, retaining the coloured prints. He dropped the envelope in the mail-chute. There was a cafeteria across the street. Eight francs bought him a glass of juice and a seat where he could see who came and went. They'd had two shots at what they wanted and had blown both but a feeling lingered that he still might have been followed. It was always possible, of course, that they might have given up, reasoning that by now he would have taken his tale to the police. Nevertheless, his feeling had been strong enough for him to employ old remembered precautions. Waiting in the Métro until the car doors were closing and then slipping out again. He had gone the wrong way through the barrier at Palais-Royal, earning the shrill abuse of the female ticket-inspector.

He finished his drink slowly and walked back in the sunlight, thinking about Suzini. The man could well make trouble for Kirstie. Something would have to be done about him.

Raven bought a Shell map of Paris and its environs at a

gas-station on the Avenue de l'Opéra. He studied the map on his way back to Ile St Louis. He found that Sully-la-Forêt was a small town sixty-nine kilometres south of the city. A key at the bottom of the map identified the principal garage as a pickup point for hire-cars. He folded the map, put it away in his pocket and closed his eyes. The noisy train rumbled on, letting in the smell of dank tunnels to vie with that of black cigarettes and garlic.

He could be wasting his time, he thought, but then he had done that before. Strange that Kirstie hadn't asked what he intended to do if and when he caught up with his quarry. It was just as well that she hadn't asked since he had no answer. He was playing each move by ear. He took another look at the batch of coloured prints, studying them in search of a clue that he might have missed. He could find none. It was hard to make sense of what had happened. Three men sitting in the Bois de Boulogne in a parked car realise that their pictures are being taken. It's of such importance to them that they're prepared to break the law to get hold of the roll of film. But *why*? It was this that intrigued him. Maybe Kirstie was right. All he was looking for was the excuse to join in the hunt again.

The water under the bridge was the colour of green glass. He crossed the street and put his thumb on the buzzer. The wicket-door was released. Madame Rambert was not to be seen but her houseplants were lined up outside her door on the cobbles, ready for their weekly soaking. He could smell Kirstie's cigarette as he put his key in the lock. She was up in the studio, sitting with her legs crossed, scanning a pile of contact-prints. He bent down and kissed her.

'OK, let's see what it looks like in the country.'

It was after two when he drove her little Chrysler into Sully-la-Forêt. The highway bypassed the small town, leaving a dramatic approach through glades of venerable oaks. Old houses standing behind extensive flower-gardens added dignity to colour and space. The stores that followed had the friendly look of the small provincial town. All were clean and well-stocked. The avenue ended in a square with trees and a bandstand. A banner, washed by rain and faded, advertised the previous year's carnival. The trunks of the trees were plastered with injunctions to vote in the forthcoming municipal elections. On the left of the square was the Shell garage, in front of them a grey and pink-washed inn with timber supports. *Hôtel de France* (*Bonne cuisine et tout confort*). It leaned away from the school next door in the direction of the *gendarmerie*, an ugly concrete building spiked with radio and television masts. A khaki-coloured utility vehicle was parked in front. Old men in flat caps sunned themselves on the benches, supporting their weight with canes. The only thing moving on the square was a large hairy dog. Raven stopped the car outside the hotel, looking across at the garage. A teenager in overalls was reading a newspaper under a parasol. A sign above his head said EUROCARHIRE.

Raven removed the ignition-keys. 'I suppose we'd better eat.'

Kirstie reached back for her purse. 'I imagine that was why you brought me here.'

He followed her into the hotel, admiring the way she moved, long-legged and rarely glancing sideways. Hyacinths growing in bowls scented the lobby. The brass gleamed and the woodwork was waxed and polished. Raven peeked into the restaurant.

'Looks good,' he said and pushed the door open.

A girl wearing a peasant apron showed them to a window-table. The menu was handwritten on mock parchment. A biographical note was printed on the cover. Monsieur and Madame Gaston Sautoy (fourteen years head chef at the *Grand Hôtel*, Val d'Isères). Madame supervised the restaurant from a raised dais, cash register in front of her, the cheese and liqueurs under her personal control. The *plat du jour* was roast leg of lamb.

Raven glanced up to find Kirstie smiling. He'd refused to eat sheep at his prep-school and the resolution had hardened over the years.

'All right,' he said cheerfully. 'You're always telling people that you never get the chance to eat the stuff. Now's the time.'

He ordered the lamb and a small carafe of house-red for Kirstie, beer and a ham salad for himself. The room was pleasantly furnished with bowls of spring flowers on the red-checked tablecloths. A man eating alone had tucked his napkin into his neckband and was showing a no-nonsense approach to the food in front of him. The windows were closed, flies buzzing behind the nylon curtains. Kirstie pinned up her hair and fanned herself with the menu.

'The French disapprove of draughts,' said Raven.

'So do Canadians,' said Kirstie. 'There's a difference between draughts and fresh air.'

'Well,' he said truthfully, 'I'm in favour of anything that gets you to put up your hair.'

She blew a kiss in his direction. The tray with their food was being inspected by Madame Sautoy. 'Clean your plate,' said Kirstie. 'These people take food seriously.'

They ate leisurely, finishing with goat cheese and coffee. Raven wiped his mouth and pushed his chair back.

'I won't be long.'

'I've heard that before,' she said composedly and lit a cigarette.

He paused at the cash-desk. 'Monsieur Castel is not there,' the *patronne* said with authority. 'He is making a retreat.'

'A retreat,' Raven said uncertainly.

A tray passed and she paused to make a note on her pad. 'The Dominican Brothers at Evreux. Monsieur Castel goes there every year.'

The man with the tucked-in napkin was using a toothpick, a cupped hand genteelly screening the operation. Raven walked across the sunlit square. The hairy dog was sleeping under the bandstand. The old men sat in silent proximity, their weathered faces betraying no emotion. Raven turned on to the garage forecourt. The youngster glanced up, holding the newspaper to keep the sun from his eyes. His hair was tinted with blond streaks and he had a bad case of acne. He showed no intention of getting up.

Raven felt the first rumble of excitement. 'I'd like to speak to someone about one of your cars.'

The youngster shook his head. 'All out, Monsieur.'

'I don't want to hire one,' said Raven. He could see a man's feet sticking out under a car in the workshop. 'It's about an accident.'

A look of caution spread over the attendant's spotty face. 'There's no one here. The boss is away. He won't be back for another week.'

The air hose dangled from a nearby hook. Raven had a strong urge to stick it under the youth's behind and blast him erect. 'What about him?' said Raven, pointing at the mechanic beneath the car.

'No.' The youngster picked at his chin. 'No, you'll have to see Monsieur Castel.'

'Look, son,' Raven said, bending forward. 'This could be a serious matter. You don't want to land yourself in trouble, do you?'

The teenager shook his head, plainly moved by the suggestion. 'I only work here, Monsieur.'

Raven tried again. 'But there has to be someone in charge. What happens when one of your cars is returned? Who does the paperwork?'

'Me. But we haven't had any cars returned. Not since the boss went away.'

Raven suddenly lost patience. 'Do you mind standing up?' he said with dangerous politeness. 'I'm getting a stiff neck standing here talking down to you.'

The attendant shambled up, still clutching his newspaper. 'A Peugeot,' said Raven and gave the licence-plate number.

The youngster's face cleared. 'Then it's not one of ours. We've got a blue Peugeot out on hire but not with those numbers.'

Experience gave Raven the answer. They must have switched plates before pulling him into the car.

'Forget the numbers,' said Raven. 'The car was yours. It had your tag on the ignition-keys.'

The attendant lapsed back into sullenness. 'I don't know anything about that, Monsieur. I told you, I only work here.'

Raven glanced round before producing a hundred-franc note. The youth's hesitation only lasted seconds. The money disappeared into his pocket.

'Who hired the blue Peugeot?' asked Raven.

'A foreign gentleman. English or American.'

'What was his name?'

'One moment, please.' The teenager went into the office, peering out from behind a display of oil-cans. He waited until the coast was clear before he came out again. He thrust a piece of paper at Raven. It was the duplicate part of the booking form.

DATE: April 27, 1980
CUSTOMER'S NAME: Joseph Ryan
ADDRESS: Pavillon Sarrault, Sully-la-Forêt
DOCUMENTS PRODUCED: International driving-licence, No. 83928, issued in Montreal, Canada, January 4, 1980
VEHICLE: Peugeot, blue sedan 5427-75
DEPOSIT: Fr. 500

Raven handed back the booking-form. 'Where is this *Pavillon Sarrault*?'

The mechanic had appeared at the workshop door and was looking towards them, wiping his hands on a rag.

'I have to go now,' the youngster said hurriedly and turned his back.

Raven returned to the hotel and paid his bill. Madame Sautoy provided the details that he needed. The *Pavillon Sarrault* was in the forest about eight kilometres out of town. Raven should take D42 behind the church. But as far as she knew, the hunting-lodge was unoccupied. She had heard that the owner was abroad. Africa, they said. Raven and Kirstie went out to the Chrysler. He pulled his map out of the glove-compartment. D42 divided five kilometres into the forest. The left fork meandered north. The house was marked. Kirstie kicked off her sandals and tucked up her long legs.

'Thank you for my nice lunch,' she said composedly.

'Why do you wear that blue eyeshadow?' he demanded.

She blew cigarette smoke through the open window. 'Because you asked me to.'

It was true but he had forgotten. 'I meant at night.'

She shook her head. 'It's not what you said. "I like that stuff on your eyes and plenty of lipstick." *That's* what you said. What happens now?'

'We'll have to see,' he said, ignoring the irony in her voice. 'We know those guys are living in the house. The kid delivered the car there. They're obviously not using the station-wagon.'

'We don't know that at all, my hero,' she said, shaking her head at him. 'It's pure assumption. How can you be sure who rented the Peugeot?'

'For God's sake,' he said. 'What do I have to have, an affidavit?' His irritation grew under her indulgent look and he was suddenly aware that the hotel proprietor and his wife were peering at them from the restaurant window. He drove across the square and parked behind the church. He switched off the motor.

Sully-la-Forêt was a lop-sided town with most of its growth lying south of Avenue Gambetta. House-tops staggered up the hill to a brand-new sports stadium. There was nothing east of the square but the hotel, school and *gendarmerie*. The forest behind encroached as far as the garden walls. The road ahead of them now plunged straight into a dense stand of beech that dwarfed the telephone poles. Hundreds of starlings perched on the line.

Kirstie claimed his attention with a mock-country whine. 'Long hair, short hair, don't make no difference once the head's blowed off!'

He raised his eyebrows. 'What's that supposed to mean?'

'You,' she said. 'It means that if it moves you'll chase it. Look at us now! Sitting in the middle of nowhere all because Superman never ends his fight for truth and justice.'

He drew a deep breath. 'I can always drop you in Fontainebleau. There's an excellent train-service to Paris. You could be home in an hour.'

'You're an insulting bastard at times,' she said.

He shrugged. 'What do you expect? First you agree to come, then you do nothing but snipe at me. Come to think of it, I don't remember any Superman jokes a year ago.' He was sorry as soon as he had said it.

The flush extended to her throat. 'That wasn't very kind,' she said quietly. 'A year ago was different and you know it.'

The search to clear her dead brother's name had involved them both on the wrong side of the law. It was the first time either had referred to it directly. He wanted to take her hand but couldn't bring himself to do it. Their eyes challenged but her anger never lasted long. She sighed.

'Why am I always the one to say that I'm sorry?'

'You're a nicer person than I am,' he answered.

She held up her hand. 'OK, you win! But if we do see these men just don't expect me to be polite to them.'

'I know you too well,' he said. 'And we may not see them. They could be anywhere.'

She manufactured a yawn and then blocked it. 'How long are we going to sit here?'

He checked his watch. 'It'll be dark in a couple of hours. We can take a look at the house. We'll go for a drive until then.'

She rearranged her hair, using a tortoiseshell pin and her hand-mirror. He watched her, grateful that they accepted one another's weaknesses as well as strengths. Children had invaded the square. The old men moved away from the invasion, stiffly, one by one. The priest's house was next to the church. Hens were scratching around in the soft brown dirt. There were no tombstones. The cemetery was outside the town limits. The children had taken over the square completely, routing the hairy dog and invading the band-stand. Kirstie put her mirror in her purse and sat up very straight.

'Action stations, my prince. Take me where you will.'

He put the Chrysler in gear and moved it forward into the forest. The ground undulated gently, offering glimpses of rabbits nibbling grass. Posted signs identified driveways. Other signs warned of the dangers of fire, deer and horses. The road forked as marked on the map. He took a left, ex-changing the hard for soft top. The winter frosts had com-pletely wrecked the surface, leaving deep potholes. A shallow stream flowed across a dip in the road ahead. Stepping-stones had been laid in it. Raven stopped and opened his door.

'Stay here. I won't be long.'

He got out before she could answer. His soles rasped on sandy soil that had blown in from the trees. Horses' hoofs had scarred the grass verge. He was nearing the bend and moved into cover of the trees. There was a stone wall with entrance-gates twenty or thirty yards away. The gates were open. A cattle-grid led to a driveway in bad repair curving through oak-trees to a hunting-lodge built of yellow stone and timber. A rhythmic thudding was coming from the house or somewhere close-by. The noise sounded like a water-pump. There was no smoke, no sign of life. Then something flashed at an upper window. He backed off hurriedly, moving deeper into cover. Once around the bend, he sprinted for the car. Kirstie was coming up from the stream, her sandals in one hand, a bunch of wild freesias in the other. Their scent filled the small car as she climbed in beside him. The car bounced over the uneven surface, avoiding the holes. Kirstie had her window down and was resting an elbow on it, fingers holding the damp tendrils of hair away from her neck.

'The house is no distance at all,' he said. 'No more than a couple of hundred yards. Somebody's watching the road with binoculars.'

'Great!' she said. 'It gets better and better.' She was drying her wet feet with tissues. She made a ball of the sodden paper and threw it out of the window. 'How exciting!'

He ignored the sarcasm and drove on to the square. The spotty-faced youth was back on the forecourt. He glanced after the car as it passed. Kirstie watched him in the rear-view mirror.

'A very unpleasant-looking young man. He's probably told them that you were in there asking questions.'

He cocked his head. 'Could be.'

She made a face. 'Know something, darling?'

He took his eyes off the road for a second. 'What's that?'

'I'd like to be about nine hundred miles away,' she said with feeling.

'North, south, east or west?' he asked sarcastically, and then relented. 'I won't get you into trouble, darling.'

Her shoulders lifted and fell. 'It's not me that I'm worried about.'

'I won't get myself into trouble either,' he said steadily.

She raised her eyes to the roof but made no reply. They drove around aimlessly, looking at a trout-hatchery, buying home-made pâté in an old vaulted barn hung with cheese and ham and patrolled by a dozen cats. The light was beginning to fade as they drove back into Sully-la-Forêt. The stores and garages were closed but the square was still lively. A couple of khaki-uniformed gendarmes were watching a game of *boules* from the steps of the police-building. Teenagers sat near the bandstand listening to music from a transistor radio. Women cooed over perambulators. Older women were shuffling off towards the church.

Raven pulled off the square and stopped at the entrance to the forest. He groped for a cigarette. Kirstie snapped her lighter, her fingers touching his wrist. The flame died, leaving her face in darkness. They could hear the noise of the square behind, the music, the shouts of the ball players. He flicked the cigarette-butt into a spiral and watched it die.

'I want you to stay in the car when we get there,' he said. 'I'll do the rest.'

Her voice was quiet. 'I'm not sure why you asked me to come in the first place.'

'That's easy,' he answered. 'I like your company.'

The church doors were open, showing people kneeling in the dim interior. Raven switched the motor on, crawling forward on the parking-lights. The motor was barely audible.

His hands were steady, his breathing normal. It was six years since he had taken the Stress-and-Strain test, scoring seven to Jerry Soo's eight on a scale of ten. The police-test exposed subjects to a series of shock experiences, assessing their mental and physical reactions. Raven had always known about fear and had always been able to control it.

He turned left at the fork. The noise of the tyres was quieter on the soft dirt. Water reflected the lights of the car. He shifted down into low and drove slowly through the stream. As the car climbed the far gradient, sky and forest were lit by an enormous flash. A blast of air took the line of least resistance, powering down the road and battering the trees in its path. Fragments of broken branches rained down on the roof. Raven trod hard on the brakes, the movement instinctive. The motor stalled. The noise of the following explosion rolled like thunder till its echoes died at last. Then the sky was dark again and the forest silent. All that was left of the explosion was its smell.

Raven wrapped an arm tightly round Kirstie's shoulders, pulling her shaking body close. His voice cracked as he tried to reassure her. She clutched his arm as a car started up in the distance. The whine of the motor changed pitch as the driver shifted gear. Kirstie wrenched herself free.

'I want to go home !' Her voice was close to hysteria. 'Do you hear me, *I want to go home* !'

'We can't *do* that,' he said gently. 'People may be hurt in there.' He switched on the headlights. Her face was tight and remote. When he spoke again she refused to answer. He drove forward, wheels rattling over the cattle-grid on to the driveway. The house showed beyond the trees. It sagged at one end, the walls torn open by the explosion. The garage was an empty shell, the rooms above it had vanished. Kirstie took her hands away from her throat.

'My *God*!' she whispered.

Raven drove on. Debris was everywhere. Two cars had been blown across the lawn, splitting at the seams. The roofs had been punched into sharp points, bumpers lopped off and scattered. There were no lights showing in the house. No flames. Nothing but darkness and desolation. He cupped his hands and shouted through them. The echo came back from the woods. He put his hand on hers and opened his door, taking the flash from the back seat. He walked forward into what must have been the kitchen. Water was dribbling from a broken pipe. There was a strong smell of gas. He tried a switch in the corridor but there was no power. He followed the beam from his flash along the corridor. The floor was littered with glass and broken picture-frames. An acrid stink clung to everything. He opened a door, looking for a phone, but found none. He picked his way back in the other direction. A room beyond the kitchen was waist-high in places with rubble and plaster. Pieces of broken slate, the bed of a billiard-table still covered with green felt, were embedded in the panelling. The Chrysler must have been a couple of hundred yards from where he was standing but he could understand why they had felt the force of the blast. The explosion had blown out the kitchen and garage taking everything in its path with it. The beam from his flash travelled slowly over the piles of rubble. Pieces of metal reflected the light. A shape caught his eye and he moved closer. A gloved human hand was sticking out of the plaster, palm upwards, fingers bent. The fabric was stained with what appeared to be printers' ink. He cleared the plaster away with his foot, half-sensing what he was going to find. The hand had been severed just above the wristbone. A fragment of bone gleamed through the coating of dark coagulated blood. He shone the flash on a piece of masonry and started pulling the debris away from the mutilated hand. There was no sign of whatever else was left of the man's body.

He made his way back to the kitchen and drank from

the dripping pipe, doing his best to blot out the memory of the billiard-room. Two of the bedrooms upstairs showed signs of occupation. Men's clothing was strewn about. A Samsonite two-suiter lay open on one of the beds. A small leather case on the dressing-table held brushes, a phial of sleeping-pills and a United States passport in the name of Kent Tyler, born Richmond, Virginia, 18 June 1943. He recognised the picture. He tried again downstairs, looking for a telephone. He found one in the library but it was dead. A Smith & Wesson thirty-eight was lying on the ground. He picked it up and sniffed the barrel. It had been fired recently. Two of the chambers were empty. He heard Kirstie calling and ran. He found her beneath an oak-tree. He sprinted across. She was kneeling beside a man lying flat on his back. A mask of congealed blood obscured his eyes, nostrils and mouth but he was breathing. This time it was the small gold lion that Raven recognised. The man's clothing was pitted with small burn-marks. His pulse was weak but regular. Raven handed the revolver to Kirstie. There was blood on her dress.

'Keep an eye on him,' he warned and ran back into the house. He found cotton, gauze and antiseptic upstairs in one of the bathrooms and filled a jug with water. Kirstie was still on her knees, holding the revolver shakily with both hands. He took the gun back and gave her the flashlamp. 'Hold the light on his face,' he instructed.

He soaked a pad of cotton in water and wiped the congealed blood away very gently from the American's mouth, nostrils and eyes. The blood was coming from a scalp wound. A missile of some sort had ploughed diagonally across the scalp, removing skin and hair without penetrating the skull. Raven felt in the man's pockets. A United States passport identified the holder as Rodney de Wayne, born in Pacific Grove, California, 1 June 1942, an actor by occupation. Raven stuffed the passport back in De Wayne's pocket.

'Get behind him and hold his shoulders down,' Raven told Kirstie. She leaned forward, leaning her weight on the man's body. The wound was still oozing blood. Raven protected De Wayne's eyes with a pad of gauze and tilted the bottle of antiseptic over the wound. He made a clumsy but effective dressing.

De Wayne twitched like a dog that dreams and opened his eyes. He pushed up painfully, supporting himself on his hands and staring straight into the light Kirstie was holding. Raven stepped back, taking Kirstie with him and making sure that De Wayne saw the thirty-eight.

'A half-inch lower and you'd be dead,' said Raven.

De Wayne's head swung towards Raven. 'I can't see,' he said hoarsely. 'The bastard's blinded me!'

SIX

HE MOVED PAINFULLY, bringing his hand away from his head sticky with blood. The smell of it was in his nostrils, its taste in his mouth. He touched the leg of the billiard-table with his shoulder. The room was in total darkness but he knew now where he was. Memory flooded back into his brain and he remembered details. Like swinging round as instinct warned him of danger – seeing the finger tightening on the trigger – the look of triumph.

Tyler had shot him with no more compunction that he'd had in shooting Scotti. They were both expendable. This was the classic cross and must have been intended from the beginning. He shut his eyes, hearing footsteps coming down the corridor. Fresh blood trickled down over his eyelids. He waited for Tyler, his heart hammering in his rib-cage. The footsteps stopped in the doorway. He heard Tyler's breathing, imagined him staring into the darkness, looking for the bodies he'd left for dead. Please God, no lights! Two quick steps from Tyler, a rustle of cellophane as something was placed on the ground. Then suddenly Tyler was running back along the corridor. The front door slammed, then the house was quiet.

De Wayne's eyelids opened through their sticky covering. Shock and loss of blood had left him weak but at least he was still alive. And then he remembered. *Jesus Christ! He was lying next to the plastic explosive!*

He dragged himself to his feet and staggered out of the

room. The light in the hall was a thousand miles away. He started the long journey towards it, time ticking in his mind. The detonating device allowed an eight-minute delay between setting and explosion. He realised now why Tyler had told him everything, boring him at times with detail. He was talking to a man he counted as good as dead. The hallway light was growing brighter. He lurched along the corridor, leaving bloody handprints on the walls. Now the door, the bright brass handle. Hurry. The hinges softly squeaking like new-born mice. Then the sweet night air on his face.

He stumbled forward, his brain ahead of his faltering legs. He reached the shelter of the oaks three seconds before the explosion. A flash as brilliant as lightning lit sky and earth. The whole world seemed to hang for a moment in expectation of what would follow. He never heard it. The rush of air knocked him off his feet into unconsciousness.

He came to his senses again, aware of someone touching him. A woman. Her breathing was shallow and he could smell the scent she was wearing. She called out loud, still staying close to him. It was easier now to put place and time together. He knew where he was and how he had got there.

He tried opening his eyes but caked blood sealed them. A man had joined the woman and was standing over him. Hope sank as De Wayne recognised Raven's voice. Then the woman had to be Kirstie Macfarlane. He was trapped unless he thought fast. *Act!* That was it. If he could bring this off, all was not lost. He lay still, hearing what they were saying but his mind back in the Carmel Playhouse.

The Monterey Examiner: CELIA WADE, PHILIP DANTZER and ROD DE WAYNE in THE LIGHT THAT FAILED. Philip Dantzer's portrayal of the blinded husband is utterly convincing. Miss Wade's Miriam is beautifully handled throughout. Rod De Wayne is good as the friend and lover.

It was four years ago but he remembered every bit of

Dantzer's business. If he ever played a role well, then let it be now.

He lay quite still, feigning unconsciousness, aware that Raven had returned to the house. Then someone was washing the blood from his face very gently. He felt a hand exploring his pockets and knew it was Raven. His passport was replaced. They knew now who he was.

The girl came behind him, pinning his shoulders down on the ground. He managed to keep his body relaxed until the raw antiseptic hit his wound. The pain was intense, as if skull and scalp were being raked with jagged metal. His wound was dressed. He sat up, eyes open, the antiseptic running down his neck. He stared straight into the light from the flashlamp. Raven's face was in shadow. He was holding Tyler's thirty-eight.

'A half-inch lower and you'd be dead,' said Raven.

It was now or never. De Wayne blinked, his voice desperate. 'I can't see. The bastard's blinded me!'

Raven's free arm descended in front of De Wayne's face but the American had been expecting it. Raven backed off a couple of steps levelling the thirty-eight at De Wayne.

'There are three live rounds in this thing and I can't miss at this range!'

De Wayne climbed up unsteadily and stood there swaying guy we jumped and you've got the girl with you!'

Raven stepped forward, jamming the gun into De Wayne's stomach as he peered into the American's face. He shook his head.

'That wound's too shallow to have done any damage.'

'It could be shock,' said Kirstie, keeping her distance.

De Wayne climbed up unsteadily and stood there swaying a little. He had to be careful not to overplay his role. He had the feeling that the girl had accepted his blindness. It was Raven he had to convince. He turned his head instead of his eyes, the way Phil Dantzer had done.

'Tyler shot us both. Scotti first, then me. Has someone got a cigarette?'

Kirstie lit one for him. He brought the right end to his

lips. Kirstie put out the flashlamp. A breeze rustled through the branches overhead. The explosion must have been heard for miles. It was a matter of time before the police located the source. He had to take off before then. Raven's cigarette glowed in the shadow.

'Where is Tyler?'

'Gone.' De Wayne's voice was bitter. 'That was his Catch Twenty-two. The bastard left Scotti and me for dead in the billiard-room with a pound of plastic explosive. I remember hearing him leave the house. God knows how I made it as far as this.'

It was Raven's teeth that showed now, lighter than his face. 'You're in a whole lot of trouble. You'd better be thinking hard. Burglary, assault and involvement in murder.'

'Bullshit!' said De Wayne. He squared his shoulders. 'I've lost my sight, man. What more can they do to me?'

'Stick you in the slammer,' said Raven. 'There's a special place for blind men. *And* you get a white cane.'

De Wayne's pulse quickened. Raven was weakening. He'd put the thirty-eight in his pocket. The breeze was stronger, chasing the cloud from the face of the rising moon.

'Look,' De Wayne said suddenly, swinging his head somewhere between the two of them. 'Why don't we talk this thing over? I need a doctor.'

'They've got those in gaol as well,' said Raven. He was almost casual, his throat within jumping distance. But De Wayne was too weak and he knew he would only have one chance.

Moonlight touched the oak-trees, laying a pattern of black shadowed branches across the silver ground. Kirstie's voice was indignant.

'What kind of a man are you, anyway?'

De Wayne gave his answer full weight. 'A man who can lay his hands on two and a half million bucks if he's given the chance.'

'Don't listen to him, John,' Kirstie said quickly.

De Wayne's voice was short of a laugh. He knew the bait had been taken. It showed in Raven's face.

'You can't afford not to listen,' De Wayne said. 'Tyler's on his way to Zürich with a bag full of forged bearer-bonds. There's no one can stop him but me. I've got all the cards, Raven, blind or not. I know every goddam move he's going to make. And you know *how* I know? Because I'm supposed to be dead, that's how I know.'

The night suddenly vibrated with the noise of a helicopter. Raven swung around, looking up at the sky. The machine was a couple of miles away, showing in the moonlight like a dragonfly over a trout-pool. Raven grabbed De Wayne's arm, forcing the American into a shambling run. Kirstie was first to the car. She took the wheel. Raven helped De Wayne into the back, followed and pulled the door shut.

'Move!' he said.

Kirstie put her foot down hard. Spray flew as they hit the stream at speed.

'Head for the motorway,' urged Raven, hanging on to the back of her seat. The car was finding every other pothole. 'If we're stopped, I'll do the talking.'

Suddenly the tyres sang on the hardtop and the lights of the town showed ahead. The square was like an ants' nest, people running in all directions; the hub of the action seemed to be the *gendarmerie*. A couple of police-cars and a fire-wagon were lined up outside. Armed cops were on the steps and the building was ablaze with lights. The crowd were spilling out into the road, forcing the Chrysler to a crawl. And then they were out of the town with Barbizon coming up with its one long street of hotels and restaurants.

De Wayne's body slumped, his head between his hands. It was Raven he had to beat and the guy was no fool. The worst was that he was probably honest. But he had to have his weak spot. They were back on N.20 with the distance poles to Paris flicking by monotonously. Every mile, every minute, was bringing De Wayne closer to safety. They drove in an uneasy silence, Raven's the only voice as he gave Kirstie directions. Another forty minutes brought them close to the Porte d'Orléans. A signal-gantry slowed them down to fifty kilometres an hour. Kirstie pulled right, taking the Paris exit. She opened her mouth for the first time in half an hour.

'Don't listen to this man, John. *Please* don't listen to him!'

Raven made no comment. They drove on into the city. People were on their way home, window-shoppers were loitering. Theatres and movie-houses were emptying on to the streets and into the late-night restaurants. A red signal held them at the intersection. Kirstie twisted round in her seat.

'I'm scared, John! Let's go to the police. It doesn't have to be Suzini.'

Traffic rumbled by, passing in front of them. De Wayne's head was still down. Bitch, he thought. She was trying to waste him. The reflection of red on the floor changed to green. Raven's voice was quiet but firm.

'Pull over to the kerb.'

Kirstie did so and killed the motor. They were halfway along the boulevard, approaching St Germain-des-Près. Across the street were the cafés patronised by writers who never wrote, painters who never painted and actors who never worked. Strobes blinked on the side-streets, welcoming tourists and dangerous riffraff to what passed for bohemian nightlife.

'Right,' said Raven. 'Now I'll tell you exactly what you're going to do. You're going to drive us back to the apartment.'

Their eyes met in the rear-view mirror. 'My god!' she said bitterly. 'I just hope that you know what you're doing.'

'I'm not sure that I do,' said Raven. 'But I know the alternative. And that's not right either.'

She sounded no more than a nudge from hysteria. 'A criminal and a lunatic! What chance have I got! Am I to understand that you intend bringing this man into my home?'

'Exactly,' said Raven. 'I want to talk to him.'

'Let the police talk to him!'

De Wayne knew that the hatred in her voice was for

him. He straightened his back. 'All I want is a doctor. There's a woman I know in Neuilly who'll help.'

'That's it,' Kirstie said quickly. 'Then we'll drive him *there*! You can do your talking in *her* apartment. I don't want him in mine.'

Raven ignored her, speaking to De Wayne. 'You'd better listen to me very carefully, chum. What happens next depends entirely on you. I want answers to my questions and they'd better be truthful.'

Kirstie put the car in gear, her face set and resentful. Ile St Louis was an oasis of silence with the dignified old houses mellowed by time standing quiet behind leafy plane-trees. Discreet doors on the dark streets opened and shut, engulfing the passer-by. Kirstie found a place to park and sat there, tapping the steering-wheel.

'You go first,' said Raven. 'Leave the wicket open and keep Madame Rambert out of the courtyard.'

De Wayne's head was averted but he could see the rebellion in her face. Her indecision only lasted seconds. She whipped the ignition-keys out of the dashboard and stuffed them angrily into her bag.

'There are times,' she said very clearly, 'when I wish to God that I'd never laid eyes on you.' She crossed the street, head high and without looking back. A crack of light in the massive doors showed that she had left the wicket open. De Wayne's long dark hair had dried in a tangled mess. The patch on his scalp was stiff with blood.

'Remember,' warned Raven. 'One wrong move and you'll find yourself on the wrong side of a cell door.'

De Wayne's smile was no more than a token. 'It's no time for long speeches. I'll behave.'

Footsteps were echoing down the street. Raven waited until they had passed. He helped De Wayne out of the car, keeping a tight grip on the American's arm. A single lamp lit the courtyard. Madame Rambert's observation-window was empty. Kirstie's voice came from somewhere inside the apartment. Raven shut the wicket gently and steered De Wayne to the right. The cobblestones were uneven. De

Wayne closed his eyes, his face registering pain. The manoeuvre added conviction to his stumbling gait.

'Three steps,' warned Raven. The elevator system clicked and the cage started its downward journey. De Wayne found himself being pushed forward. A door was opened up on the fifth floor. The American waited in the small hallway while Raven pulled the kitchen curtains closed.

'In here,' Raven said from the doorway. De Wayne stayed where he was. 'Here!' Raven said again.

De Wayne groped his way forward towards the kitchen. Raven took his hand and led him to a chair. Raven poured a couple of glasses of scotch and placed one on the table.

'Drink that, you probably need it.'

De Wayne was living his part. It was a matter of auto-suggestion. Faced with the lie-detector test he had convinced himself of his innocence. Now he was blind. He raised his head in Raven's direction, careful that his eyes never followed a moving object.

'What is it?'

'Scotch-and-water or maybe you shouldn't with a head injury.'

It was difficult to tell from Raven's expression whether or not he had swallowed the bait completely. De Wayne's sun-tanned fingers felt for the glass. He raised it carefully to his mouth and drained the contents.

'There's enough in this for everyone,' he said. 'Don't let the girl talk you out of it.'

Raven was leaning against the dresser. 'I don't get talked out of things very easily. Or, for that matter, into them.'

De Wayne's face was haggard in the artificial light. 'There's no sense us bullshitting one another, Raven. You're a man of the world, you've been around. This is worth over a million dollars to you.'

Raven smiled as though remembering something that pleased him. 'You'll have to do better than that, my friend. You see, I happen to have all the money I need. And, well, you know – I cheat a little here and there with my taxes.'

'OK,' said De Wayne. 'Look, you think what you like

about me. It's not important. But I certainly didn't kill anyone. All I did was turn thief in fast company and I got roasted.'

'An occupational hazard,' said Raven. The elevator cage was clattering up the shaft.

'Look at it this way,' De Wayne said urgently. 'Suppose you touch me off, what do you get out of it? In any case, what do you think the police can prove without my testimony?'

They were on the top floor. Kirstie put her key in the lock. Raven glanced back out on to the landing but she went straight into the bedroom and slammed the door hard.

'You broke into this apartment and you put your bloody hands on me,' Raven said grimly. 'I don't like it.'

De Wayne covered his closed eyes with his fingertips. 'One question. Have you been to the police or not?'

'You're in trouble whichever way,' answered Raven.

De Wayne let his breath go. 'Just what *is* your angle. You must have one. How did you find the house?'

'I used to be a cop,' said Raven. 'And I have an inquiring mind.'

Shock spread from De Wayne's brain to his body. 'Jesus *Christ*!' he said feelingly. His mind raced to his rescue. Everyone had his price. The trick was to determine it. 'Why didn't you turn me over to the police in Sully? Why bring me here?'

Raven leaned back again; this time it was against the wall. 'I'm not quite sure. For one thing, I don't care about the law in the way that you probably think that I do.'

De Wayne slowly raised his head. 'Then what the fuck *do* you care about?'

Raven nodded as though to himself. 'A good question. But I think I know the answer to that one. The eternal verities.'

' "The eternal verities"!' De Wayne brushed at his eyes again. 'What are you, some sort of religious freak? There has to be *something* you want and don't have. With two and a half million bucks I can make most dreams come true.'

Raven moved to the other side of the table, sat down and craned forward. The television was on in Kirstie's bedroom.

'You'd never understand. You've got the wrong sort of mind. The sort of things I like are knocking a rook out of the sky with a twenty-two rifle. Putting salt on the tails of people like you. But now that I've got you, I don't want you any more. And I'm not too sure that the police are the answer. I just don't know what to do with you. Therein lies my difficulty.'

De Wayne's chin lifted. His voice was soft. 'A hunter! I've got myself a goddam hunter. It's Tyler you want, isn't it?'

Raven nodded. 'That's right. It's Tyler I want. I want him to have that money in his hot fist and then pull the plug on him. No more, no less.'

'And what happens to me?' asked De Wayne.

'You?' Raven shrugged. 'I don't really give a shit about you.'

'You mean I get none of that money?'

'Not one penny,' said Raven. 'I'm letting you go in return for certain information. And don't for one moment think that I'm turning you loose before I'm completely satisfied that you're telling me the truth, the whole truth and nothing but the truth. So help you God!'

De Wayne exhaled noisily. 'You drive a hard bargain.'

'The man double-crossed you,' said Raven. 'Left you for dead. So see how it ends. He goes inside and you walk the street free. There's a lot of satisfaction there even though you're blind and without the money. I don't call that a bad bargain. I'll give you two minutes to make up your mind.' He turned his wrist and looked down at his watch.

'How can I be sure?' asked De Wayne.

Raven's shoulders moved again. 'I'd say a couple of hundred people must have asked me the same question. I'll give you the same answer. You *can't* be sure. It's a chance that you have to take.'

'You got it,' De Wayne said with sudden hoarseness.

It was after ten-thirty when he finished talking. The

information he had given was mostly accurate. The omissions were his insurance.

'He needs to send cables to New York and Düsseldorf, get the answers back. He can't go near the bank with those bonds until Friday. Show yourself before then and he'll be off and running.'

Raven put his pencilled notes away in his pocket. 'I never show myself. I've been in the game too long.'

The kitchen door suddenly burst open. Kirstie's face was white under the freckles. Raven went to her quickly.

'What is it, what happened?'

She shook her head, unwilling to answer. 'Tell me!' he insisted.

'It was on the news,' she said. 'The explosion, everything. They found the body of a man blown to pieces, burned and unrecognisable. They're looking for an Englishman who was making enquiries about the *Pavillon* this afternoon. They showed that boy from the garage, talking to the police.'

'Did they mention the car?' Raven asked quickly.

'No, but what the hell does that matter? I'm scared, John.'

'It'll be all right,' Raven said automatically.

She broke away, her face furious. 'It will *not* be all right! I asked you to take that man to the police and you refused. OK, do whatever you want with him but get him out of here.'

'Listen,' he said, reaching for her again, but she avoided him.

'The hell with listening!' she retorted. 'What am I supposed to do, stand here wide-eyed while you put everything that we have at risk? I'm getting sick of your one-man crusades. What right do you have to *do* this to us? What goddam right do you have?'

'He's going now,' Raven said quickly. 'I'm going to need your help again with Madame Rambert.'

'You need my help for nothing,' she said bitterly. 'And in any case Madame Rambert's gone to bed.'

Raven lifted his hands, then let them fall. 'There's no

sense at all talking to you when you're like this. All I wanted ...'

She gave him no chance to continue, her mood changing to one of entreaty. 'Look, John. I realise that I'm the one who got you into this and you have the right to play your own hand. But I want you in one piece, goddammit, unharmed. *Please* go to the police!'

'I can't,' he said simply. She slammed the door but not before he saw the tears in her face.

He picked up the kitchen phone. 'What's your girlfriend's number in Neuilly?'

De Wayne muttered the digits. Raven dialled and waited for the ringing tone, then put the receiver in the American's hand.

'It's Rod,' De Wayne said quickly. 'Don't ask questions, listen! There's been an accident and I need help. I'll be with you as soon as I can.' He groped for the stand and replaced the receiver.

'How do you know that she'll be there?' asked Raven.

'She'll be there.' It was an act of faith.

'Whose apartment is it?'

'Some chick Fran worked with. She's away. Fran's there alone.'

'How do we get in? What floor's the apartment on?'

'The first.' De Wayne produced two keys on a ring. 'They lock the entrance door but one of these opens it.'

Raven dropped the keys in his pocket. 'On your feet!' He steered De Wayne into the hallway. The bedroom door opened and Kirstie appeared.

'A bloody crusader,' she said bitterly. 'And of course it won't stop here.'

Raven's grip was firm on De Wayne's sleeve. 'I don't understand you.'

'You understand only too well. I have some news for you.'

'That's great,' said Raven. 'But it'll have to wait.'

'I just called Ed Hovic at the American Hospital.'

He looked at her with sudden anxiety. 'You're not sick, are you?'

She shook her head. 'I asked about your friend. "A tangential wound to the scalp inflicted by a high-velocity missile." '

Raven was still hanging on to De Wayne's sleeve. *'What?'*

She nodded at the American. 'Ed says its classic, something called "transitory cortical blindness". The pupils may look perfectly normal but you can't see a thing. Vision *always* returns. I thought the news might make you feel better. *Both* of you!'

The two men moved out to the landing. 'Don't talk,' whispered Raven. 'And count the stairs as you go. There are eight to each flight.'

The overhead lamp was burning down in the courtyard. Madame Rambert's quarters were in darkness. Raven slipped the wicket-lock and pushed De Wayne out on to the street. Moonlight was reflected in the swiftly running river. He unlocked the Chrysler and strapped De Wayne in the passenger-seat. The American leaned back on the headrest and closed his eyes. He was round third base and sprinting for the home-plate.

He kept thinking about the gun in Raven's pocket. The ex-cop seemed to have forgotten that it was the murder-weapon. De Wayne lurched sideways as the car swerved into the Arc de Triomphe free-for-all. Traffic was still quite heavy. He opened his eyes, hearing Raven's voice.

'What did you say the name of the bank was?'

'The Landesbank,' De Wayne said wearily. 'It's on Alfred-Escherstrasse.'

Raven held his speed and course steady as a police-car flashed past. They were approaching Neuilly, a neighbourhood of middle-class apartment-blocks set on leafy roads between the river and the Bois de Boulogne. Raven started reading the street-names.

De Wayne spoke carefully. 'Tyler has a nose like a hounddog. If you jump the gun with the bank, you'll lose him.'

Raven swivelled his head around briefly, smiling. 'You worry too much about me, my friend. I've no intention of jumping the gun.'

A street-sign showed ahead. Raven turned the car on to a driveway. The condominium angled the corner. Trees and pool were floodlit. Some of the apartments were in darkness but most of the windows were illuminated. Raven stopped outside the entrance.

'We're home. What's the number of the flat?'

'One B. It's on the left as we go in.' De Wayne opened his door and felt for the ground with his feet. 'Transitory cortical blindness.' Good old Ed Hovic, whoever he was.

Raven unlocked the door to the red-carpeted lobby. Gilt chairs flanked a Chinese urn bearing dried flowers. The lift-cage was decorated with fat-bottomed cherubs. It was very quiet.

The door to One B opened before they reached it. The woman standing in the doorway was elegant in velvet pants and a white silk shirt. The lines in her Slavic face seemed to be cut with a surgeon's knife. She took De Wayne's face in tender hands. He stared back blindly, resisting the urge to wink. She whirled suddenly, snarling at Raven like a bobcat.

'What have you done to him?'

De Wayne grabbed her arm. 'It wasn't him, honey. It was Tyler.' He felt his way to the sitting-room and found the suede-upholstered sofa. Raven stood in front of the fireplace. The furniture and paintings seemed to fascinate him. The woman was standing behind De Wayne, her hands kneading his neck-muscles. He reached up and held her wrist.

'Make coffee, sweetheart!'

'Not for me,' Raven said hurriedly. 'I'm on my way.'

A ten-carat aquamarine flashed as Fran lifted her hand to her brow. 'Is someone going to tell me what happened?'

'Tyler shot us both,' said De Wayne. 'The Italian's dead.' He lit his first cigarette in a long time.

Fran's eyes were on the bulge the gun made in Raven's wind-cheater. He moved an arm awkwardly.

'It's not as bad as it looks. He'll get his sight back. I wouldn't advise going to a doctor. He'll tell you why.'

DONALD MACKENZIE

'The law,' De Wayne explained. 'The high times are over, baby. Goodbye, Costa Rica. It's the deal I've had to make.'

Raven looked at his watch. 'I have to go. You're on your own. I'll keep my end of the bargain. My advice is to get him out of here the moment his vision returns.'

'And Tyler?' Her eyes had the glittering brilliance of a jewel.

Raven zipped up his wind-cheater. 'I'm taking care of Tyler. You could call it a sort of sudden-death arrangement. Don't worry about it.'

Fran followed him to the hallway. The front door opened and closed. De Wayne raced along the passage, holding his finger to his lips. He looked through the optic-glass spyhole and saw the Chrysler pulling away. Then everything was quiet again.

Fran cradled his face in her fingers, shaking his head from side to side with a mixture of anger and relief. Then she started to laugh.

'You bastard!'

He put his palm over her mouth. 'Is the car downstairs?'

She nodded and he took his hand away. 'Get your things together fast. We've got to make Zürich tonight. *Move!*'

He inspected his wound in the bathroom mirror and removed the soiled dressing. Blood was still oozing but he plugged it was a couple of plasters. He washed his hands and face. There was nothing he could do about his clothes for the moment. He went into the bedroom. Fran's coat was on the bed. She was pulling the last strap on her bags.

'Where's the book?' he demanded. She pointed at the dressing-table. He put the South African passport in his pocket. They'd laughed at him in Milan. Six passports he'd bought, and four driving-licences. He must have been psychic. He combed his hair over the sticking-plaster.

'This is bad shit, Fran,' he said over his shoulder. 'Scotti was a racket guy. We're going to have to move fast.'

She carried the two bags as far as the front door and came back. 'You mean they'll be after you?' she demanded.

He nodded. 'Where's the gun?'

90

She showed him the small automatic in her bag. He looked around the room for the last time.

'Bad shit,' he repeated. 'Those guys in Milan don't know Tyler. They know me. The bastard covered all the angles.'

She shrugged into her doeskin coat, her face troubled. 'And the money?'

A smile built on De Wayne's face. 'Ours,' he said. 'Every goddam nickel of it. Nothing and nobody is standing in our way now.'

They left the flat, carrying a bag each, and took the lift down to the underground garage.

SEVEN

RAVEN DROVE THE CHRYSLER around the corner and turned through the first set of gates. The beam from the headlamps picked out the lettering on the board sticking out of the grassy bank.

He stopped under a plane-tree, cut his motor and lights and wound down the window. A frog was croaking in the undergrowth over by the swimming-pool. His manoeuvre had brought him back close to the condominium. There were no walls between, nothing more substantial than strands of wire strung from tree-trunk to tree-trunk. He counted the windows left from the entrance-hall. The lights in One B were still burning. He used a match for his cigarette, trying to remember if the curtains had been drawn or open. They were closed now. A silhouette showed briefly. He leaned forward, looking across at the apartment. The pool furniture had been stacked. The pennants fluttered from their poles. Peace in bourgeois Paris. Doubts floated through his mind like a feather always just out of reach. There was nothing tangible, nothing he could put his finger on, no more than a vague suspicion that somehow he had been had. The woman had impressed him as being tough, intelligent and totally devoted to De Wayne. Another survivor. You couldn't use conventional yardsticks to judge people like that. They were a breed apart, amoral rather than immoral, with the fierce defensive loyalty outcasts show for one another. She'd probably move De Wayne out of town the moment his sight returned. They would surface somewhere else, thousands of miles away, the lure of easy money under their pillow wherever they slept.

He lit a fresh cigarette from the butt of the old one. Maybe that was the source of his uneasiness. De Wayne had gone in deep, only a touch away from a violent death, with two and a half million dollars at stake. Yet he'd surrendered without really fighting. Raven had a strong suspicion that this was out of character. A car sounded and Raven raised his head. Headlamps swept through the trees as a car emerged from the ramp leading up from the underground garage. It slowed and turned on to the condominium driveway. Raven sprinted for the street and flattened himself against a tree-trunk. The convertible came out fast, a blue Jaguar with a tan top. De Wayne was driving with the woman sitting in the passenger-seat. He looked ten years younger and was smiling. Brake-lights glowed, then the car was gone. Raven started to run to the Chrysler, then thought better of it. He wouldn't last five minutes if he tried to tail De Wayne. There was a certain sour satisfaction in proving that his hunch had been correct. De Wayne had been conning them from the moment he opened his eyes.

He drove back fast to the island and let himself quietly into the apartment. A crack of light showed at the bottom of Kirstie's door. She was sitting up in bed, wearing her lace-trimmed nightdress. Her hair was neatly brushed, her face fresh and without make-up. He put the car-keys and claim-ticket in the dish on the dressing table.

'It's in the garage at the end of the Quai. We'd better leave it there for a few days.'

She was reading *For Whom the Bell Tolls*. She kept her place, offering her cheek as he bent to kiss her.

'You mean in case the police have the number,' she said meaningly.

He sat on the edge of the bed, hoping to delay the argument that he sensed would surely come. The gun sagged in the pocket of his windcheater.

'De Wayne conned us,' he admitted. 'He left half an hour

ago at the wheel of a convertible.' He told her what he had seen.

'So what happens now?' There was no suggestion of I-could-have-told-you-so in her voice.

He blocked a yawn and went up to the studio. He came back carrying the Airlines Annual and started leafing through the flight schedules. He glanced up after a couple of minutes and found Kirstie watching him.

'I know,' she said quietly. 'We're going to Zürich, right?'

Raven nodded. 'De Wayne's already on his way there. Look, these people have pushed paperhanging into a million-dollar racket. I've got to see the end of it, Kirstie. Try to understand.'

She put her book down on a side-table, the gesture emphasising her seriousness.

'It's better that I *don't* try to understand. All I need to do is keep praying.'

He shook his head but made no reply. Her smile was sad. 'There are times when I find you very hard to take, John Raven.'

'Don't wrestle with it,' he said jokingly. 'There are times when I find myself hard to take.'

She continued to stare at him and he finally lowered his eyes, tracing the pattern of the patchwork quilt with his forefinger. It had taken him thirty-nine years to find what he had with her and here he was, in danger of seeing it slide away, unwilling or unable to do anything about it He raised his head again, seeking forgiveness.

She was seven years younger than he was in age but light-years older in wisdom. Her smile broke gradually with a tenderness that embraced him.

'You're a selfish unprincipled shit, John Raven,' she said.

He shook his head, grinning. 'A shit, maybe and certainly selfish. But unprincipled never!'

He lifted the phone and called the Air France night-service. The first flight to Zürich left Charles de Gaulle at eight-zero-five in the morning. He gave the employee a credit-card number. The clerk confirmed that the tickets would be waiting at the airport. Then he called a car-hire firm and arranged for transport to the airport and booked an alarm-call through the operator. He brushed his teeth, switched off the light and lay down beside Kirstie.

'I ought to tell you that I love you,' he said, staring up at the ceiling.

Her hand found his and gripped it hard. 'A selfish un-principled shit,' she repeated.

EIGHT

TYLER FOLLOWED THE COURSE of the stream, the weight of the bag forcing him to move lop-sidedly. The grassy banks were steeper now, giving way to firmer ground, and the beeches were sparser. Water splashed somewhere on his left. There was enough moonlight filtering through the foliage to see the Range Rover on the rocky outcrop ahead. He leaned forward into the climb, his shirt sticking to his back, the noise of the explosion still ringing in his head. He was up in the clearing now, where the source of the stream bubbled out between boulders. The Range Rover stood there stark, solid and utterly trustworthy. A shovel and water-drum were strapped to the bodywork. He unlocked the car and switched on the radio, fiddling until he had found the local news-station. He put his bag behind the seat and picked up the clothes he had left there. A brown tweed jacket and cord trousers replaced his blue flannel suit. A raincoat completed his new outfit. He drenched the suit with petrol, carried it twenty yards away and touched it off with a match. The fabric burst into flames. He dispersed the ashes with his foot. He was washing his hands in the spring when he heard the noise of the helicopter. He raced down into the trees and stood there with his heart banging. The machine clattered into the moonlight, outlined by its riding-lights. Tyler flattened himself as the aircraft banked sharply before veering out of sight. The noise of its motor gradually decreased.

There was no doubt about it being a police helicopter. The markings were distinct. A few minutes earlier and they'd have seen the flames from the burning suit and would surely have investigated. His stomach churned at the thought. He couldn't afford to make another mistake like that. The further he removed himself from the scene the better. Even a hundred miles could make all the difference. Once across the border into Switzerland, there'd be nothing to connect him with either of the two dead men.

He climbed back into the Range Rover and took a long swig of beer. There were four more bottles in the refrigerated bag and a package of sandwiches. His escape route had been etched on his brain for weeks. He pushed the ignition-key home and turned it. The motor sang sweetly. Gauges registered a full fuel tank, the right oil-pressure and a working electrical system. He switched on dimmed headlights and drove down into the forest, keeping to the secondary trails. Half an hour found him twenty miles away on the network of poplar-lined roads that ran to the east. He joined the Basel motorway at Langes, stopping in the centre of town to mail a letter at the main post-office. The envelope was addressed to Henry Petersen, c/o Chase Mutual Inc., Bärengasse, Zürich. Inside was the Republic of Eire passport with its Costa Rican visa. Another hour and he was driving through the forbidding streets of Belfort. The radio was playing, newsflashes interrupting the hard rock music. The newscaster spoke of a hold-up in a Paris jewellery-store, of miners trapped half a mile below the surface, a multiple car-crash. The announcer's voice droned on. An explosion had taken place in Sully-la-Forêt. A man's body had been found. Foul play was suspected and the police were looking for an Englishman. A *man's* body! Why not *two* men? And who the hell was the Englishman? He swung left beneath the gloomy citadel on to the Altkirch highway, driving with more confidence now in spite of his night-blindness. Traffic was thinner and every yard took him closer to safety.

The road switchbacked for fifty miles, then the lights of

St Lous showed ahead. A long straight street led directly to the French and Swiss frontier posts. He dimmed his lamps and joined the line of vehicles waiting to be processed. The beer was gone and his mouth was suddenly dry. De Wayne's face flashed into his consciousness. The guy had always been rock-firm under pressure. Tyler unwrapped a stick of gum and let the car roll forward a few yards. He was a foreigner leaving France in a British-registered vehicle. It wasn't the Customs he was worried about but the passport control. A cop in a dark-blue uniform stuck his head into the cab.

'Vos papiers!'

Tyler handed over his passport. The cop carried the document to a lighted window where a colleague sat. The passport disappeared through the guichet. Tyler shifted the wad of gum. His identification was being checked against the WANTED list. He was sure of it. No more than another hundred yards to go but it seemed so far. That was a risk that had always been calculated since the pay-off was in Switzerland and the frontier had to be passed at one point or another. De Wayne had sworn that the Milan passports would stand up to any sort of inspection. The next few minutes would tell. He went on chewing his gum. The cop was coming back, his face expressionless. He pushed Tyler's passport forward.

'Allez, Monsieur. Roulez!'

Tyler drove the Range Rover across the stretch of no-man's-land into the Swiss Customs zone. Grey uniforms replaced khaki and blue. The flags and faces were different, the procedure the same. It was almost eleven o'clock. The lights were bright both inside and outside the austere stone buildings. The Swiss border control barely glanced at Tyler's identification, waving him through perfunctorily. He was sweating again, profusely, driving into the prosperous surburban streets. Basel was a city that used its wealth discreetly, without flamboyant display. It was twenty years since he'd been there but he had forgotten nothing. He'd been at school at the castle on a mountain overlooking the Rhine fifteen kilometres away. Memories flooded back as he drove downtown. The girls he had squired to Sunday tea-dances *Chez Singer*. Groups of singing teenagers, arms linked, stamping down the snow to make sled-runs. He remembered swimming the cold green river to Germany and back. But the best memory of all was lying under the cherry-trees with the smell of new grass in his nostrils. It was the one time in his life when he'd been really happy.

The Basel he recalled had changed. The skyline was broken by towering buildings made vulgar by the old grand beauty still standing on the banks of the river. Bahnhofplatz with its hotels and transport terminals was busy in spite of the hour. The Turks, Greeks and Yugoslavs who worked in the city congregated in front of the Central Station, exchanging news and gossip.

Tyler drove into an all-night garage. An attendant hurried out of the office. Tyler gave him the keys to the Range Rover and clambered out with his bag. The attendant gave him a claim-slip.

'May I ask how long you'll be leaving your car? It makes a difference where I park it.'

Tyler copied the man's lilting Swiss German. 'About three weeks. I'm going on a walking holiday.'

He put the slip in his pocket and carried his bag past the lighted hotel façade into the station. By the time anyone got around to being curious about the Range Rover he'd be four thousand miles away. It was after eleven but the station concourse was still crowded. Everything worked like a Swiss watch, quietly and efficiently. Even the baggage was moved electronically. He bought a first-class ticket to Zürich and a copy of the *Herald-Tribune* from the news-stand. Two men he'd seen earlier over by the booking-office had broken up, drifting apart to take new positions near the barrier at the end of the tracks. One was in *lederhosen* and carried a rucksack. The other looked like a farmer but Tyler smelled cops. It wasn't easy to think of want or crime in this land of prosperous law-abiders. Yet Switzerland was a target for high-flying crooks of all kinds and nationalities. In order to protect themselves and their guests, the Swiss had developed a well-trained and well-equipped police-force with a reputation second to none.

Tyler made his way to the waiting express and found a window-seat. He was alone in the car. He put the bag on the floor with his feet resting on it. He checked the financial page of his newspaper. General Chemical bearer-bonds had taken a hike of two points since the previous day's trading. The two cops were still at the end of the track, scanning each passer-by. One operated from behind a well-used map, the other just rocked on his heels and smiled vaguely. Tyler lowered the blind. The train left dead on time with a farewell blast of the whistle for the city it was leaving. The express might have been running on billiard-tables. Its progress was without jar or vibration. Tyler closed his eyes. Tomorrow would be a busy day. He was using the office of Chase Mutual as base. The two banks were within walking distance. If all went well he'd be through by the afternoon.

He dozed off and was awakened by the altered pitch of the wheels on the rails. The train was beginning to slow. It was five to one by his watch. He raised the blind. The lights of the first Zürich suburbs showed beyond the rain-spattered windows. The train jolted to a stop. Its arrival was announced from speakers somewhere up in the roof of the concourse. There were no porters in sight, few people meeting the train. He made his way to the side exit. A single cab stood on the rank, a Mercedes with a cigar-smoking driver.

Tyler put his bag on the ground. 'Do you know where Emtal is?'

The driver nodded.

'Will you take me there?'

The driver reached back, unfastening the rear door. 'Seventy-five francs.' Tyler climbed in. It was a quarter past one in the morning.

The Bahnhofstrasse pavements were wet and deserted. It was a street for the rich with no concessions made to the impecunious. A sable coat draped on a model was priced at eighteen thousand dollars. A discreet card mounted on a tiny easel carried the consoling message QUALITY LASTS LONG AFTER THE EXTRAVAGANCE IS FORGOTTEN.

The driver turned his cab left at the end of Bahnhofstrasse and then right. Whatever nightlife was left was centred on the narrow streets beyond Bellevue Platz and the pick-up bars along the quays. The lake was half a mile wide at this point, the lights on the opposite shore obscured by the thin slanting rain. The windscreen wipers flicked steadily. They drove past stolid-looking houses surrounded by stone walls and dripping trees. The streets were as silent as the hills that rolled behind them. Eighteen kilometres out of the city they exchanged the lakeshore highway for a mountain road that climbed up through dripping fir-trees to a sodden expanse of pasture-land. The farmhouses were dark and isolated, fronted by vats of liquid manure. Dogs barked as the headlights lit the barns and outbuildings. They were thirty-four kilometres out of Zürich, eight hundred feet above the lake and several hundred years behind in terms of living. The two farms were unchanged since the days of the confederation, give or take a few pieces of machinery. A building loomed out of the mist. The fields behind stretched into wet darkness.

'Here!' said Tyler.

The driver braked. The headlights shone on a wooden chalet surrounded by an ugly wall built of stone and iron piping. Water ran from the guttering. The shutters were closed. Not a single light showed in either of the two farms. Tyler gave the driver his seventy-five francs and added ten more.

'Thanks for your trouble.'

The man pocketed his money, glancing across at the chalet. He opened his mouth for the first time since they had left Zürich.

'You'd do best to come back with me. I'll give you the ride for free.'

The rain fell softly on Tyler's neck and shoulders. 'I'm only here for a couple of days and it's better when the sun shines.'

The driver shrugged and made a tight U-turn, tyres hissing on the wet hardtop. The sound of the motor drifted back up as the Mercedes began the descent to the lake.

Tyler pushed the iron gate open. There was a concrete path that was breaking away at the edges. It divided. The right-hand branch led to the garage, the left to the rustic porch and front door. He put his bag down and let himself into the hallway. The small chalet belonged to a forty-two-year-old spinster who worked as a dietician for the Canton of Zürich. Her sole outside interest was the study and collection of wild flowers. The chalet was furnished with the leftovers from the family's city apartment. Table, chairs and sofa in the sitting-room were in the Swiss tradition, hideous and solid. The carpets were well-worn. There were few decorations other than Fraülein Seiler's displays of dried flowers. The impression given was that this was no place to seek comfort. Mountain air, the fields and sturdy shoes were all that mattered. The owner's father had built the chalet and she used it for two months a year. July, Christmas and Easter. Hers had been the first letter in reply to Tyler's advertisement in the *Zürcherpost*.

AMERICAN AMATEUR BOTANIST SEEKS CHALET WITHIN EASY REACH OF ZURICH. GARAGE ESSENTIAL. GOOD PRICE PAID FOR TWO MONTHS' RENTAL. BOX 1072.

He'd bought a second-hand Volkswagen and driven up to Emtal on a fine early April morning. The fields had been steaming gently in the weak sun. Bells clanked around cows' necks. The smell of the manure pits was sharp and strong. Mists hid the lake below. He inspected the chalet from the outside. Its location was perfect. The school was no longer in use and according to the bus-schedule in the shelter there were three runs a day in either direction. An appendage added the information that bus-conductors would collect and deliver mail. Emtal was no more than forty minutes' drive from the city yet completely isolated. He sat on the wall for a while, looking across the fields to the fringe of fir-trees. After a few moments he was aware that he was under observation from the nearest farmhouse. He walked down a track spattered with cow-droppings. The woman was standing in her doorway, unabashed at having spied on him. She gave him the glass of water he requested. She was middle-aged and plain and listened to his queries about wild flowers with the cautious tolerance of someone dealing with a case of mild lunacy. Tyler thanked her heartily, drove back to Zürich and called Fraülein Seiler at her work. They met over tea at the *Baur-au-Lac Hotel*, exchanging cash and a signature for the keys to the chalet.

He switched on the light and opened the bedroom. The entire chalet smelled of wet dog. Fräulein Seiler's labrador was an explorer of the deepest recesses of the forest. The clothes Tyler had left were on the bed together with a pig-skin attaché-case and the Belgian twenty-two automatic he had bought in Hamburg. He used the flashlight from the kitchen to check the garage. The black Volkswagen was precisely as he had last seen it, three weeks before. It was almost a quarter to two. He undressed in the stuffy bedroom and put out the lights. Being up here shrouded in mist gave him a feeling of security. No one in the whole wide world knew who or where he was. Drab and uncomfortable as it was, the chalet was going to be his last resting-place on the way to Costa Rica. He was under no pressure. He'd realised right from the start that there was only one way of handling De Wayne. The guy had the nose of a fox. His sense of smell had to be blunted. The only way to do that was to open every drawer and show him what was inside. Dates, places, the mechanics of converting the forged bonds into real money. Everything had to be exposed. The Italian's removal had always been understood between them. It was ironic to think that the next bullet had been for De Wayne himself.

Tyler yawned and turned on his side. The mattress and pillow were hard but he slept soundly. Sunshine pierced the shutters and woke him. It was a quarter to seven. He opened the shutters at the back of the house, leaving those at the front closed. He made himself breakfast in the kitchen with the heady mountain air coming in through the window. The bread and milk he had left in the freezer were in perfect condition. It was eight o'clock by the time he had shaved and dressed. He picked up the telephone and dialled. The number answered immediately.

'Südwest Verein. Good morning, may I help you?'

'Kent Tyler of Didrixon & Loeb. I'd like to speak to Mr Halbrecht, please.'

Halbrecht's English was brisk and heavily accented. '*Ja*, Mr Tyler! Good morning, how are you? Welcome to Zürich.'

Welcome indeed. Tyler looked at himself in the mirror. Brooks Brothers charcoal-grey suit, Racquets Club tie, black moccasins. 'I'm fine, thanks. I'd like to see you some time this morning if that's possible. I have the bonds with me.'

'Of course,' Halbrecht said quickly.

'General Chemical,' Tyler went on. 'The current issue, maturing in six years' time. That's the five-thousand-dollar unit.'

'That should be all right,' said the banker. 'How many do you have?'

'Five hundred,' answered Tyler. 'There's no question of us relinquishing the bonds, of course. We're simply putting them up as collateral.'

'Understood,' said Halbrecht.

'We agreed on a thirty-day loan based on the current market value, OK?'

'One moment, please.' Halbrecht was obviously using his desk-calculator. 'There was the matter of an inter-bank transfer if I remember correctly.'

'Right,' said Tyler. 'I ought to mention that this is a new account, Mr Halbrecht. New York thinks highly of it. We've promised funds by four o'clock this afternoon.'

'There'll be no problem there,' assured Halbrecht.

Tyler's confidence was growing by the second. 'I wouldn't

want any slip-up. Chase Mutual's European director is in town.'

'Don't worry.' Halbrecht said quickly. 'We can advise by telephone and send a certified cheque by messenger. It would help if you could give me the name of Chase Mutual's bank here in Zürich.'

'Laudesbank, Alfred-Escherstrasse.'

'I will have the documents ready for your signature,' Halbrecht promised. 'I assume that you have your power-of-attorney with you, Mr Tyler.'

'Sure,' said Tyler. On paper it was a good deal for the bank. They charged twenty per cent for a short-term loan, which would be in the region of fifty thousand dollars. They were in a highly competitive business and a minimum of time was wasted on a deal once it was closed. The bonds were safe for months.

It was Halbrecht again. 'Would half past eleven suit you, Mr Tyler?'

'Half past eleven will be perfect,' said Tyler. 'I'll look forward to seeing you.' That, he thought, had to be one of the understatements of all time.

He put the power-of-attorney in his pocket together with the Petersen passport and driving-licence. The coming interview was simple. He'd handled bigger transactions for Didrixon & Loeb and he was trusted at Handelsbank.

He'd been sitting in the Investors Club in Zürich only a couple of months before, watching the stock-market quotations on the television screens and chatting to one of the investment counsellors. She was as pretty as she was bright and he'd taken her out for a drink. They'd dined together and she'd told him of a remark that she'd overheard. The speaker had been Paul Halbrecht on the subject of Tyler. 'A young man going places in a hurry,' had been his verdict.

He stacked the bonds neatly in the attaché-case, relaxed and confident. They were every bit as good as the originals. There were no ghosts in his world, no past, only the future. He made his way out through the kitchen and opened the garage. The Volkswagen started easily. Sunshine transformed the plateau. Wood-smoke wreathed from the farmhouse chimneys. The massive snowcapped Alps rose majestically fifty miles away. The road descended through dark silent fir-trees. The ferries were out on the lake, taking passengers into the city from the towns and villages along the shores. White waves showed in the cold green water.

Everything was different by daylight, like a Swiss Tourist Board poster. Order, prosperity and *gemütlichkeit*. Cows waddled with fat swinging udders, the lush meadows were bright with spring flowers. Neat wooden houses overlooked Alpine-turf lawns. Tyler was completely at ease as he had always known he would be. 'The balls for the big one', they'd said in the army about him. They were wrong then but they would have been right now.

The *Pavillon Sarrault* would now have been overrun by cops dusting-off for fingerprints, popping flashbulbs, going through the rest of their usual antics. And all for nothing. What they'd find would be the pieces of two Male Caucasians as the jargon had it. And the assumption would be that he was one of them. His clothes and the passport he'd left would support the deduction. Identifying De Wayne might take longer. No, his plan was working perfectly. There'd only been one rocky moment and even that had turned out to be a false alarm. There'd been a whole lot of satisfaction in blowing a hole in De Wayne's brainpan. It was like driving a stake through Dracula's heart, destroying the one person who made him vulnerable.

It was almost ten o'clock when he drove up Alfred-Escherstrasse. Downtown Zürich had been at work for two hours and the pavements were thronged with affluent shoppers, polite people and unhesitatingly honest. Tyler drove the Volkswagen on to a short narrow street running between the two rivers that fed the lake. A parking-place was painted CHASE MUTUAL INC ⸱He left the Volkswagen there and climbed the steps. The Seeturm Building soared above the swift shallow Limat River, its glass walls reflecting the sun like mirrors.

The lobby was decorated with Mayan motifs. There were

no shops, none of the bustle of the North American office-building, no incentive to loiter. An express lift ghosted Tyler to the fifteenth floor. The offices were at the end of the sunlit corridor where a large picture window offered an end-on view of the crescent-shaped lake. Bronze lettering on a door spelled out the name of the company. Tyler opened the door.

He had taken a three-year lease on the suite, furnishing it at O. B. Grauweiler, 'The office of tomorrow for use today'. Mechanical devices monitored the intake of light, heat and oxygen. The typewriter table rose and fell electric-ally. There was a telex machine, photocopying unit and a closed-circuit television set that linked the office with the Bourse. The reception area had a glass-topped table littered with prestige magazines and behind it a comfortable sofa. He had bought space in *Swiss Current Affairs*, *The Investors Chronicle* and *The Business World*. Chase Mutual's credit-rating had already been established thanks to Didrixon & Loeb. The announcement in the journals touted neither for business nor funds. *Chase Mutual Inc.: Lead Managers of Eurobond Issues.*

The door to the inner office opened. The short-haired blonde was still tanned from skiing and was wearing a blue-and-white linen dress. Her fingers flew to her mouth as she saw Tyler.

'Mr Petersen! I'd no idea you were here. You gave me a shock!' Two years as an au pair in Belgravia had given her an upper-class accent in English.

Tyler smiled pleasantly. 'I'm sorry about that, Miss Clausing. I just flew in from New York. I should have let you know I was coming.'

The flush faded from her sunburned skin. She moved forward with athletic grace.

'But what a shame! ˇ mean, I could have made all the arrangements for you. There's little enough for me to do as it is. I feel that I'm earning my money under false pretences.' There was a hint of coquetry in her manner, a suggestion of areas that might be open to his exploration.

He had noticed it before and turned it to his advantage. He excused himself glibly.

'It was pretty much a last-minute decision. We're setting up something quite important. How are you, anyway?'

He held her at arm's length, inspecting her. She showed good teeth in a smile.

'I'm fine, thank you.'

'And the work?'

She gestured at a pile of stapled files on a side-table. 'Another ten days should see it finished. I can't really say that I'll be sorry.'

She followed him into the inner office. He put the attaché-case down on the floor.

'I know how you feel but don't worry about it, Miss Clausing. There'll be a lot of exciting things for you to do from now on. Travel, for instance. How do you feel about that?'

Her smile was shyer this time and her cheeks coloured again. She opened the curtains. The windows looked out across the lake to the undulating hills, the pine and fir forests above. The white peaks of the Alps appeared in the distance, remote and mysterious.

Fox-hunting prints hung on the walls. On the desk was a silver-framed picture of a woman with two children. Tyler had found it in a Düsseldorf photography-store. Fraülein Clausing turned the picture to better advantage.

'I hope your family is well,' she said primly.

'In great form,' he said easily. 'And looking forward to coming to Zürich. Is that all the mail?' The letter he had posted from Langes was at the top of the pile.

The girl's voice was awkward. 'I'm afraid it is, Mr Petersen. The cables were addressed to you personally so I didn't open them.'

'Good,' he said, smiling. He had sent the cables himself, to give the venture a more convincing ring of veracity. 'We'll be taking on another girl next week. Someone to do the boring work. You'll be more of a personal assistant.'

She coloured again, obviously pleased. 'The tapes are on your desk. Will that be all, Mr Petersen?'

'That'll be all,' he said, and came to the door with her. Each play of the game had been calculated. 'I'll tell you what – I'm expecting someone here for a conference. Why don't you take the day off? Call your boyfriend and make him buy you lunch.'

She shook her head. 'This is Switzerland, Mr Petersen. We just don't *do* things like that.'

'More's the pity,' he said, and took her raincoat from the hook. He collected her bag and gave them both to her. 'Boyfriend or not, I don't want to see you until eight o'clock tomorrow morning. Good*bye*, Miss Clausing.'

He waited, smiling, until she disappeared into the lift. Then he locked the door and drew a long deep breath. De Wayne had always criticised the Chase Mutual set-up. But nothing was a waste of time or money when two and a half million dollars were at stake. An attachment to the telephone recorded all calls. He played the tapes through. They were banal enough. An enquiry from the Zürich Chamber of Commerce, an office-cleaning outfit soliciting business, routine calls without interest. He opened the letter he'd addressed to himself and extracted the Republic of Eire passport. He put it away in the Bogner safe next to the first-class Swissair ticket. The name on the ticket was the same as that on the passport, Joseph Mangan. The passport bore a Costa Rican entry visa valid for three months. Once there he was assured of a permanent stay. His picture was on the title-page. The ticket was open. If the business at the bank went as smoothly as he hoped it would he'd be able to take off at eleven-fifteen the following morning. If not, he'd catch the Saturday-morning flight. Swissair had guaranteed his seat and Mexican Airlines offered a daily connection with Costa Rica. He closed the safe.

Südwest Verein was a private bank with a seat on the Zürich Bourse and links with the textile and brewing industries. Paul Halbrecht had dealt with the Didrixon & Loeb account for the past seven years. The bank premises were in a four-storeyed building on Bärengasse, a weathered stone house with a bear rampant carved above the entrance. Tyler mounted the steps, carrying his attaché-case. It was eleven-twenty-seven. He gave his name to one of the two receptionists and took a seat in a creaking leather sofa. The interior of the building was modern with open-plan facilities for customers and staff. The banking hall had black marble pillars and floor. Greenery and house-plants grew in every place possible. The entrance to the strong-rooms showed beyond the mahogany counter. A double set of bright steel gates guarded the short escalator. There were no more than a dozen customers, relaxed and chatting to the tellers. The security guard was reading a newspaper. There was an air of impregnability about the place. Here was a temple to conservative banking where the word 'risk' was anathema. The phone buzzed on the girl's desk. His receptionist stood, trim and smiling.

'Do you want to follow me through, please, Mr Tyler?'

The lift took them to the second floor. Halbrecht was waiting at his office door, a robust, soberly dressed figure with a ready smile and cold slate eyes. The top of his large head was bald. He seized Tyler's hand and shook it effusively, accenting every other word.

'Good *morning*, Mr *Tyler*! How *nice* to *see* you!'

He closed the door with his foot and indicated a chair, still beaming. 'Please sit down, Mr Tyler. May I offer you some refreshment? Tea or coffee, perhaps? Or something a little stronger?' The smile was even wider.

Tyler placed his attaché-case on Halbrecht's desk. He shook his head. 'Nothing, thanks. As a matter of fact, I'd like to get this business concluded before the New York market opens.'

Halbrecht's face sobered. 'I understand perfectly, Mr Tyler. I have the documents ready for signature.' He put his thumb on a button.

The paintings on the walls were of the type popular in South Germany and Switzerland. Stylised oils done in bright colours and featuring chamois perched on rocks against a

110

gothic background. Halbrecht leaned back in his chair pressing his fingertips together.

'Herr Frascati is our bond expert.'

Someone knocked on the door. 'Come!' said Halbrecht. Frascati was in his forties with the face of a highly intelligent rat. Deepset eyes of exceptional brilliance were divided by a long questing nose.

'Mr Tyler of Didrixon & Loeb,' said Halbrecht. Frascati's handshake was deferential. 'So,' said Halbrecht. 'Shall we proceed?'

Tyler clicked the two locks and lifted the lid of the attaché-case, hiding his mounting excitement. He extracted the first sheaf of bonds from the Bank of America envelope and passed it across the desk.

'They're in batches of fifty.'

Sunshine streamed through the windows, brightening the room and its sombre furnishings. Halbrecht counted methodically, his fingernail scraping on the slightly greasy paper.

'*Fünfzig,*' he said, and passed the bonds to Frascati. The younger man's hands were well-kept with long spatulate fingers. He took one of the bonds, snapped it perfunctorily and held it to the light. Then he started to count. Tyler broke the seal on the second envelope. He watched Frascati's face for the first sign of suspicion but the interest of both men was clearly in numbers. They checked the contents of the last envelope. Halbrecht glanced down at his desk-calculator.

'Five hundred?'

'Five hundred,' Frascati agreed. He was bending forward, enclosing the bonds with his forearms as a dog guards a bone with his legs.

'Two and a half million dollars,' said Halbrecht.

'There is one problem,' Frascati said slowly.

The words formed in Tyler's brain. *These bonds are forgeries.* He felt the sweat, cold on his ribs.

Halbrecht frowned. 'Problem? What sort of problem?'

Frascati's long nose quivered. 'The valuation. Do we take

the New York quote or ours? There's a difference of point zero five.'

'Aha,' said Halbrecht, looking pleased. 'Herr Frascati is a stickler for details.'

Tyler spread his hands. 'We'll take the Zürich quote. It makes things easier for everyone.'

Frascati rose in a shaft of sunlight, a Venetian merchant satisfied that his wealth has been well-placed.

'Then I shall take the bonds down to the vaults,' he said protectively. He wheeled in a small four-wheel trolley from the next room and loaded it. He made a little bow in Tyler's direction and left.

Halbrecht slid the two documents across the desk. 'So, Mr Tyler. If you will just sign here and here. Perfect! And the power-of-attorney, please. We must make a photocopy.'

He put the notarised form on top of the signed papers. '*Ja, gut!*' he said comfortably. 'Now how do you wish this transfer to be made, Mr Tyler?'

Tyler shrugged. His brain was cool and collected. It was his body that wanted him out of there fast.

'Our account with Chase Mutual is in dollars. Why don't we keep it like that? It simplifies the book-keeping. I'm lunching with one of their people. When can I tell him that they will be credited?'

'Ah!' said Halbrecht, and took another look at the clock. 'In about ten minutes' time. Do you happen to know who takes care of the Chase Mutual account at Credit-Union?'

Tyler shut his empty attaché-case. 'Herr Asbek.'

Halbrecht made a note on his pad. 'I'll call him immediately. We'll send confirmation round by messenger.'

Tyler rose to his feet. His legs felt oddly spry. This was almost the realm of fantasy, of wealth created by pure belief.

'I'll be in touch with New York this evening. The partners will be grateful, Mr Halbrecht. We couldn't have swung this deal without your help. Thank you.'

Halbrecht walked him to the elevator. 'Goodbye, Mr Tyler. Remember that the bank is always ready to help valued clients. Goodbye!'

Tyler's last glimpse of Halbrecht was of the man leaning forward looking earnest and showing his teeth. The lift dropped to street level. He walked out into sunshine and strolled east, giving himself time. He'd wait half an hour before he called Asbek. The narrow street was jammed with cars on both sides. A visitor had put his convertible up on the Seeturm car park. A blue Jaguar with French TT plates. Tyler let himself into the office and locked the door. He stood at the windows looking down. Sailboats were out on the lake below. A water-skier in a rubber suit leaned into a slalom turn leaving a wake of white horses behind. Tyler smoked a couple of cigarettes, pacing himself deliberately. It was twenty past twelve when he called Laudesbank.

'Chase Mutual Incorporated, Petersen speaking. I'd like a word with Herr Asbek, please.'

'*Mr* Petersen!' Dick Asbek, Institut Selig and London School of Economics. Bachelor, customers' man and going places. He'd made it very plain that doing business with Chase Mutual was going to be a pleasure. 'I can guess why you're calling. Don't worry, everything is in order. The Didrixon & Loeb payment is in. I've literally just put the phone down, trying to call your office. Do you want the exact figures?'

'Yes,' said Tyler. It was unnatural not to show an interest in money. He could still see the lake from where he was sitting. Sun and water were somehow brighter.

'It's in dollars,' said Asbek. 'Two million two hundred thousand. Do the same instructions hold good?'

'You have them in writing,' said Tyler. 'I need the money in cash before Saturday.'

Papers rustled at the other end of the line. 'That's right,' said Asbek. 'But we weren't sure of the exact amounts.'

'OK,' said Tyler. 'So this is how it goes. Four banker's drafts, dollars, Swiss francs, D marks and yen. Each for half a million dollars and the rest in cash. Dollars again, the biggest bills you have.'

'Right,' said Asbek briskly. 'You can pick them up after lunch.'

'There's no particular hurry,' said Tyler. 'Later on this afternoon will be fine.'

'Half past two,' promised Asbek. 'I'll have everything ready by then. Do you want a guard from the bank?'

'That won't be necessary,' Tyler said quietly, and put the phone down. It was a pity that the moment could not be shared. You start from scratch and make a dream come true, letting nothing stand in your way. And suddenly the dream is there, clothed in reality, and there's nobody to applaud.

He took the Mangan passport and air-ticket around the corner to the Swissair offices. A girl confirmed his flight for the following morning. He intended to drive straight to the airport from the chalet. Seven hours later he'd be in Mexico City. Piaf had regretted nothing and he knew what she meant. He'd do the whole thing again if he had to. Marriage, murder, had left him untouched by the canker of compassion. The rogue elephant was always better than the herd.

He ate a sandwich and drank a glass of wine on a terrace overlooking the lake. It was twenty minutes to three when he reached Alfred-Escherstrasse. Laudesbank was a larger bank than Südwest Verein, impersonal yet with an air of energy and dedication. Shirt-sleeved tellers worked behind bullet-proof glass. TV screens showed the latest market quotations. A tape-machine clattered out its messages. A girl showed Tyler into a small room with windows staring out at Bahnhofstrasse. Asbek was there almost immediately, tall and sandy-haired with pink-tinted spectacles. He placed a large envelope on the table between them.

'If you'd like to count that, Mr Petersen. We've given you the largest bills that we had.' He smiled and pushed a receipt in Tyler's direction. Most of the bills were thousands. Tyler put them in his attaché-case.

'And the banker's drafts?'

Asbek looked slightly embarrassed. 'I'm afraid that's my fault, Mr Petersen. The vice-president in charge of that section went home at noon, a funeral. But they'll be ready first thing in the morning. I could bring them round to your hotel by eight-thirty or come to your office. Whichever you prefer. I can only apologise. I took it for granted that Herr Schiffli would be here.'

Tyler stood up, hiding his frustration. 'I'll be here at eight-thirty. Just make sure there's no slip-up. A lot of things are hanging on this deal.'

'You can depend on that, Mr Petersen.' Earnestness had replaced Asbek's easy manner.

'Eight-thirty then,' Tyler said significantly. He made his way back to the Seeturm Building, locked his office door and washed his face and hands. He brushed his short white hair, looking at himself in the mirror. The strain was beginning to show in his eyes. He'd have to be careful. Another glimpse of the contents of his attaché-case reassured him. There *was* no need to worry. The bonds were buried in the vaults and the transfer had been made. He could even have asked for the whole sum in cash without provoking too much suspicion. The appearance of the Arabs in Europe had made this sort of transaction commonplace.

He wrote a note and left it on Fräulein Clausing's desk. *Have gone to Geneva. Will call you on Monday or Tuesday. P.* He locked his flight-ticket and the Mangan passport with the money in the attaché-case. He was on his way out when the telephone rang. He picked up the receiver.

'Chase Mutual Incorporated!'

He heard the instrument being replaced at the other end of the line, not brusquely but gently. He put his own receiver down. Someone getting a wrong number. He carried the attaché-case down to the Volkswagen, fastened his seatbelt and took the right lane for the lakeshore highway. A breeze was ruffling the water, filling the sails of the dinghies that were out. He drove carefully, his mind on the following day. The two-hour stopover in Mexico City allowed him to deposit three of his letters-of-credit with the Royal Bank of Canada. His connecting flight for San José took off at seventeen hundred hours. He'd no doubt that he'd be met by someone from the Ministry of the Interior. General Varela's price-of-entry was half a million dollars in cash.

He turned off at Durnau, taking the mountain road. The

DONALD MACKENZIE

Volkswagen climbed up steadily into clearer air. The road wormed through still fir-trees. The breeze had dropped. Sound travelled clearly. A car was following, a couple of bends behind. Conifers gave way to lush pastureland. The fields were empty except for browsing cattle, swinging their tails at the flies as the Volkswagen drove by. The narrow ribbon of hardtop looped through the hamlet. Tyler drove through the open gates and was halfway into the garage when the car behind came into view. He recognised it immediately. It was the blue Jaguar convertible that had been parked outside the Seeturm Building.

He dropped the garage doors and stood there in the dark, listening to the sound of the Jaguar's exhaust die in the distance. He let himself into the chalet and went through into the bedroom. He sat down, wiped his forehead and neck and picked up the small automatic.

NINE

THE TELEPHONE RANG and De Wayne reached for it. The operator's voice was professionally brisk and cheerful.

'Good-morning! Your seven o'clock call. Breakfast is on its way!'

Someone tapped on the door. De Wayne rose on an elbow. 'Leave it outside!'

He slipped out of bed and tied a towel around his middle. There was a pot of coffee, orange juice and croissants and a copy of the *Zürcherpost*. He relocked the door and carried the tray across to the bed. They had driven hard from Paris to be delayed by an overturned truck and a tail-back a couple of miles long. They reached Zürich at one o'clock in the morning and tried three hotels without any luck. They found the *Europa Motel – TV and Kitchen Facilities* on the road out to the airport, a sprawling complex with strobes and a dirty pool. Ten minutes would take him into the city or out to the airport.

Fran was still asleep, lying on her back with her head on one side and parted lips. He shook the bed gently.

'Fran, honey, it's seven o'clock! The breakfast's here.'

She awakened immediately, without moving her body, eyes fixed on him with a cat's awareness. Then she looked round the room. The shadow of a passing car appeared on the ceiling. A trick of light coming through a chink in the curtains reduced the image to the size of a toy. Fran swung her long dancer's legs to the floor and went to the bathroom.

He heard the familiar routine, the clearing of the throat and the gargling. He had finished his croissant by the time she came back, sweet-smelling, with her kimono tied and her hair brushed. He pushed the tray across the bed and looked at his watch. 'It's twenty past seven. Tyler will be up by now, getting himself ready for the day's work. Not a care in the world.'

She sat with her legs tucked up under her, frowning at him over the top of her coffee-bowl.

'Know something? You worry me. You keep telling me what he's doing and what he's thinking. How can you be sure that he's even up there in this chalet?'

He parted the curtains. A discoloured lawn with untended flower-beds stretched to the airport highway. Whoever did the gardening had given up the struggle. The Jaguar was parked right outside the window with the top up. De Wayne turned, lean and tanned.

'I don't believe it,' he said, shaking his head. 'I mean, what kind of a question is that?'

Her Slav face was obstinate. 'He does this, he does that! I'm asking you how you can be sure.'

He tapped himself on the chest. 'I'll tell you why I'm sure, Fran. Because that fucker had no need to lie to me! He could afford to tell the truth. As far as he was concerned I was already dead. Don't you see that, Fran?'

'No,' she answered flatly. 'Not the way you see it, anyway. He's going to be jumping at shadows. Those people in Milan will be looking for him. You said so yourself.'

He poured himself the last of the coffee. 'I said something entirely different. Scotti's friends never heard of Tyler. They don't know his name even. *I'm* the one they're going to be asking questions.'

'Great,' she said bitterly. 'Well, I don't like it. Tell me something, Rod. How many times have I asked you to do something for me?'

He put the tray outside the door and turned to face her. 'You haven't asked me for a goddam thing. Not once in four years. That's why I want the best for you. That and because I love you.'

'Please, honey,' she urged. 'I never expected life to turn out like this but I don't regret a thing. It's just that I'm getting bad vibes. Why don't we take off, keep going? There's still something left of the money you asked me to hold, the expense money he gave you. And we could sell the car.'

He looked at her, remembering the loyalty he had always demanded. Not once had she failed him. Why the hell didn't she understand?

'You mean take off and run?' he demanded. 'Run from *who*? From *what*, Fran? Look, I knew that Scotti was going to get it. *Sure* I knew! I'd have pulled the trigger myself. The guy was an ape and this was a chance in a lifetime. What we're talking about here is that Tyler was supposed to be my friend. The bastard tried to kill me. For money.'

She let her breath go, her ice-blue eyes troubled. 'I don't care about money.'

He laughed. 'You don't? When was the last time I saw you eating grits and gravy? Bullshit, Fran! You care about money. But you want it brought to you by Brinks with an affidavit that it's one-hundred-per-cent kosher. Well, let me tell you something, Fran. That money's there and it's ours.'

'We can work,' she said obstinately. 'We've done it before. We always made out.'

'I just don't believe what I'm hearing,' he said. 'Sure we made out! Living in crummy apartments with roaches sharing our meals. Bums pissing in the alleyways. Living on peanut-butter and jelly sandwiches!'

'I want you alive,' she said.

'Jesus *Christ*!' he exploded. 'You're looking at me as though I've got the mark of death on my face! What *is* this, Fran? Look, do what your heart tells you. Take the next flight back to Paris and wait for me. I'll be in touch, never fear. You're a compulsive habit. There's nobody else and there never could be.'

She slid from the bed. In spite of the lateness of their

arrival she had hung up her clothes. There were trees in her shoes. She buttoned through the striped dress and inspected the backs of her stockings in the mirror.

'I'm going nowhere without you,' she said. 'And you know it. But it doesn't mean to say that I like it.'

He kissed her cheek and went into the bathroom. Cold needles of water stung his body. He shaved in the shower, spluttering, and dressed in the same burn-pitted slacks and sweater he had worn on the previous day. The clean shirt was one that he had left in Fran's apartment. She had tidied the bed and the dressing-table and was sitting by the open window.

'Two and a half million bucks!' he said, slapping cologne on his face. 'Tyler's going to get it and we're going to take it from him. And there's not a goddam thing he can do about it.'

She turned troubled eyes. 'How about the other guy, the ex-cop?'

He used the coarse comb on his hair. 'You think I'm crazy? He doesn't know about the chalet. And his time-table's wrong. He thinks the action is tomorrow. No, honey. Raven's the least of our worries.'

'That's what I like,' she said wearily. 'A man of decision. It'll be a consolation when I'm sewing mailbags or whatever women do here in gaol.'

He sat down on the edge of the bed, took her hands in his and forced her to look at him.

'Do you think I'm some kind of a yoyo or what?' he demanded. Their eyes met. After a while she shook her head. He continued to hold her wrists. 'Then *listen* to me, Fran! Tyler's going to be walking into that bank with the bonds in an hour or so's time. And he's going to make it, Fran, no two ways about it. Those bonds are perfect. You're not dealing with some con-man walking in off the street. What you have here is a man the people in the bank know and trust. Can't you see, Fran? They've been *waiting* for him to bring in this deal. It was all arranged, more than two months ago.'

Her eyes flicked sideways at the mirror as though for some form of reassurance.

'The money goes from one bank to another,' he continued. 'There's this dummy corporation he's got, Chase Mutual. The money goes into their account and Tyler whips it out in cash. I'm talking about the best part of two and a half million bucks, Fran.'

Doubt clouded her face. 'Two and a half million in cash?'

He moved his shoulders impatiently. 'That's right. Cash, negotiable securities. Banker's drafts. Whatever. He was talking about Certified Deposits at one time and they're just as good as bearer-bonds. The bastard's walking on air by now. He doesn't know a goddam thing about Raven and I'm dead.'

The tip of her tongue touched the corner of her mouth with the delicacy of a mosquito alighting. 'We know how *he* gets the money,' she said. 'What I don't understand is how *we* get it.'

A man in a straw hat wandered by with a rake on his shoulder. De Wayne closed the window and sat down on the bed again.

'We stay on his tail, that's how. Look, he doesn't know you from a hole in the ground so you're the one who will tail him. Once he goes back to the chalet, I take over. As soon as it's dark I move in.' He took the gun from the drawer, stuffed it into his belt and smoothed his sweater over it.

She cried rarely and even then as often as not from temper. But this time the tears came with sadness. He wiped her eyes with a handkerchief, soothing her.

'Come on now, honey. It's not going to be the way you think. I ought to kill the bastard but I won't. All I want is that money. That'll be enough to cripple him for life. I'll fix things so that we get the start we need. In any case, there's not a goddam thing that he could do.'

She sniffed hard, blinking. 'Do you remember the first time we met. You quoted poetry at me, no less! *"Had I concealed my love and you so love me longer, since all the wise reprove confession of that hunger . . ."* Dedadedadeda!

121

A romantic, I thought. You were smoking dope with that Sausalito poetess and you told me that the bitch wrote it. I mean I really *felt* that poem. It was a year before I learned that it wasn't our flat-chested friend who wrote it but Elinor Wylie. You bastard.'

'She couldn't even find a rhyme for suck,' he said, and his smile faded. 'We can do it, honey. It's just one day in a lifetime and from then on it's whatever you want. You're the one who'll call all the shots.'

It was her turn to smile. 'I got to know my Elinor Wylie. *"Liar and bragger, he had no friend except a dagger and a candle and . . ."* It could have been you she was writing about. I love you, Rod. Why don't we let it go at that?'

He nodded. 'Sure. Yeah, that's right, Fran. Why don't we let it go at that?' He glanced at his watch. 'We'd better move. The banks open at eight. There's a parking-place in front of the Chase Mutual building. That's where we'll go.'

He loaded their one bag into the boot of the Jaguar, drove round to the office and checked out. The man in the straw hat started the sprinklers. De Wayne took the wheel and donned the dark-lensed glasses. Fran was already wearing hers. He slipped the gun from his belt to the glove-compartment.

'It's going to work, sweetheart,' he promised. *'It's going to work!'*

It was almost eight o'clock when he drove on to the See-turm forecourt. He avoided the stencilled parking-spaces, pulling into the Visitors area. The entrance steps to the office-building were about fifty yards away and facing the front end of the Jaguar. De Wayne lit a cigarette.

'He's six-two, well-made with short whitish hair. No hat. At least, I never saw him wear a hat.'

Cars were pulling on to the car park, passengers joining the flood of pedestrians flowing across from the street. De Wayne kept his eyes fixed on the entrance-steps. There was only one way into the building. Behind it was the river. Minutes passed. Eight o'clock. Eight-fifteen. The flood now was no more than a trickle. Fran and De Wayne had exchanged places. She was sitting up very straight, her hands firmly fixed on the wheel, staring out across the lake.

'*That's him!*' said De Wayne. 'The Volkswagen.' Tyler was getting out of the car, elegant in the morning sunlight, a bulky attaché-case clutched under his arm. He started to thread his way through the lines of parked cars. The direction he had taken was bringing him close to the Jaguar. De Wayne went down under the dashboard. 'Take a good look at him!'

He stayed down with his head between his knees until he heard her voice. 'He's gone. I saw him take the elevator.'

De Wayne straightened up and put his dark glasses on again. He pointed up the street.

'He'll be going to that bank on the corner. Whatever you do don't lose him when he comes out.'

She turned her face towards him, eyes blank behind the dark glasses. 'Do I stay in the car?'

'Fran!' he pleaded desperately. 'If he drives you follow. If he walks you walk. Just stay out of sight but *follow*!'

She drew a deep breath. 'OK. Where are you going to be?'

He pointed again. 'I'll be somewhere on that bridge. Now have you got that straight? If he comes back here to the building, you wait for him to come out again. Whichever way it is, car or on foot, you follow him.'

'You got it,' she said shortly.

He opened the door on his side and leaned back through the window. 'I love you, honey. Stay loose!' He reached over, swivelling the rear-view mirror so that he could see his reflection. He rearranged his hair to cover the dressing on his scalp. He needed a cap or some other sort of head-gear.

He hurried down the street. There was a wharf below the bridge, the starting place for trips round the lake. A line of people were buying tickets for the white-painted excursion-steamer. Hucksters were peddling balloons and paper-windmills. Children clustered near a candy-floss stand. He pushed his way through the crowd and up the steps to a point on the bridge where he could see both the Handelsbank and the Jaguar. The entrance to the Seeturm Building was just out of sight. De Wayne was doing his best to appear inconspicuous but he was aware of an elderly couple staring at him. He touched his hair self-consciously. It was his clothes, probably. He needed more than just something for his head. The man was wearing an alpaca jacket with knee-breeches and clutching an *alpenstock*. His partner had on the sort of uniform popular with mature Swiss women. Grey hair, dress and grey shoes with a patent-leather sheen to them. They continued to stare and he turned his head. They were watching a double-scull skiff on the river below. De Wayne moved away self-consciously and sat on the balustrade, swinging his legs. Nerves.

His plan was simple, to take every nickel that Tyler collected, clean the fucker out. It was tempting to think about blowing a hole in the bastard's head but he'd promised Fran. Not only that, it would be too dangerous. The best thing to do would be wrap a rope around Tyler, fix it so that he wouldn't be going anywhere in a hurry. They could call the police later, just give the address and hang up. He and Fran could be in France five minutes later. Doubling back on their tracks was ace thinking. They'd simply stroll away from the Jaguar and take the *rapide* for Paris. Another six hours and they'd be home in the States, make their move from there. Brazil or Mexico. It would have been a real charge to have turned up in Costa Rica but Tyler had contacts there. California wouldn't be safe for too long. The gentlemen from Milan would be sharpening their knives, unwilling to accept the popular version of Scotti's passing. The trouble there was that they knew too much. They had provided the passports and he'd had to tell them why he needed Scotti. These guys weren't Mustachio Petes. They were businessmen in silk suits, working out of executive suites. But the end-product was still the same. Hung up on a meat-hook somewhere with an assortment of lead in your stomach.

He slid down from the balustrade, seeing Tyler coming down the street carrying his case. Tyler went into the bank. De Wayne hurried below to the wharf, mingling with the crowd outside the steamship-office. He had a better view of the bank entrance from here. It was half an hour before Tyler emerged, still clutching his bag. Instinct told De Wayne that it was empty. Tyler started back towards the Seeturm Building. De Wayne followed thirty yards behind. The street was busy and it was simple to stay covered up. In any case he had a strange feeling of superiority, as though the figment of his death had given him a cloak of invisibility. Tyler's white head bobbed along in front. He crossed the street to the ramp. His course was taking him perilously close to the Jaguar. De Wayne hoped to God that Fran was playing it cool. None of those long hard stares that had burned the Pacific Grove Johns who used to hang around the stage-door.

De Wayne trotted on to the forecourt, pausing briefly behind a Mercedes Limousine. A ginger Chow rose stiff-legged on the rear-seat. De Wayne moved on. Tyler was at the top of the entrance-steps, going through the glass doors. De Wayne made his way to the Jaguar. Fran had the newspaper from the motel open in her lap. She couldn't speak a word of German, let alone read it. But she was playing the role for her life.

De Wayne's voice betrayed the rush of adrenalin. 'He's laid the bonds on them. He'll be out again. Remember what I said, Fran. Keep him in view but stay out of sight.'

She folded the newspaper deliberately. 'Keep him in view but stay out of sight. That's brilliant, De Wayne.'

'Just do it,' he pleaded. 'If he walks I'll stay on the Volkswagen. If he drives, we ride together, OK?'

She nodded, using her hand-mirror to repair her make-up. 'You look great,' he said quickly. 'Just don't overdo it. This isn't Vegas. And listen. If for any reason we're separated, there's a ticket-office under the bridge. That's where we meet.'

She put her mirror and lipstick back in her bag. If she was feeling the strain she showed no sign of it. De Wayne retreated to the far side of the forecourt. The cars near the ramps running down to the street were parked much closer there, offering more cover. He kept his eyes firmly fixed on the Jaguar. A minute or so later, the door on Fran's side opened. She emerged, tucking the side-pieces of her sunglasses into a head-scarf. Her coat was slung round her shoulders. Jesus *Christ*! Bacall in a Bogart movie. What in hell did she think that she was doing!

He had to wait for some time before he saw Tyler, a good way ahead, still carrying the attaché-case. He was walking purposefully, looking straight ahead. There was no hint that he suspected that he was being followed. Then suddenly both Fran and he disappeared. De Wayne took the opportunity of examining the Volkswagen. The inspection did little for him. There was nothing to see on the seats and the glove compartment was closed. The speedometer-clock had a reading of fifty-one thousand two hundred and sixty kilometres. The doors were locked and the tyres muddy. De Wayne walked back to the bridge. A man in a chef's cap was selling beer and frankfurters from a wagon. De Wayne bought both and sat down on the river-bank. If Tyler came from the opposite direction, it would have to be by way of the bridge overhead. It would still be easy to spot him.

Half an hour stretched to an hour. There was still no sign of either of them. De Wayne walked the length of the street and back, staying close to the wall, his senses on stalks. It did him no good. It was gone half past two when Fran appeared, strolling leisurely across the forecourt. She was still wearing her sunglasses but not the head-scarf and she was carrying her coat.

He hurried up the street to intercept her, grabbed her from behind and swung her round by the arm. 'Where's Tyler? What in hell kept you?'

She waited until he took his hand away. 'Staying out of sight, that's what kept me. He's in there!' She nodded at the glass entrance-doors.

He hurried her across to the Jaguar. 'This thing sticks out a mile,' he muttered, and moved the car thirty yards. They sat for a moment, challenging one another.

'For *Crissakes*, Fran!' he burst out. 'What *happened*?'

She closed her eyes briefly and moved her shoulders. 'I had this vision. You were going to be waiting. You'd say something like "Fran, you were great!"'

'*Fran!*' he pleaded. 'It isn't the time to get touchy.'

She opened her eyes and looked at him, shaking her head. 'I guess not. You're not going to change at your time of life. Well, his first stop was Swissair. No hesitation. He knew exactly where he was going. He was there for about seven minutes, then he went to the *Pam-Pam*.'

'The *Pam-Pam*,' De Wayne repeated.

'That's exactly right,' she said. 'It's a cafeteria-type place with a terrace overlooking the lake.' She affected to think. 'He had a sandwich and some kind of a glass of wine. I was inside like looking through the phone-book. Then he went to the bank, the Laudesbank. He couldn't have been there for more than twenty minutes. Then he came back here.' She glanced down at her arm, rubbing the marks his fingers had made.

'You were ace,' he said quickly. 'That means that he's collected the money. All we have to do now is follow him home. That won't be difficult. He has to take the lakeshore highway and the traffic is heavy. We'll be able to give him plenty of room. He turns off about ten miles out of town. The chalet's a couple of thousand feet up in the mountains. You drop me where the road branches off.'

She looked at him, stroking the base of her throat with the tips of her fingers.

'And I follow him to the chalet, right?'

'Right,' he said. He lit a cigarette, one eye on the entrance to the office-building. 'But you don't stop, you keep going. There's a ring road that brings you back to the lakeshore highway. You come back to where you left me.'

There was no time for her to answer. De Wayne slid down on his shoulder-blades as Tyler came through the glass doors and crossed the forecourt to the Volkswagen.

'He sure looks worried,' said Fran.

De Wayne peeked. '*You'd* look worried if you were carrying that kind of money. Let's get going. And keep your distance. We know where he's heading. All we want to do is make sure that he goes there.'

Grey-blue smoke puffed as the Volkswagen started. Its hunchback shape showed five cars ahead. They kept the same distance as they skirted the sparkling water. More sailing-dinghies were out, the billowing colour of their sails perilously low above the ruffled waves. Signposts and petrol-stations flicked by, the villas on their wooded slopes. De Wayne leaned forward, peering through the windscreen.

'It's coming up now,' he said pointing. 'Next to the Domecq sign.' A cut-out of a Spanish bull menaced the grass slope. A depression showed in the hillside where the mountain road sliced up into fir-trees. The Volkswagen swung right, its roof-top showing as it started its climb.

'Let me off here,' said De Wayne. Fran swerved right and braked. 'I'll be somewhere around here,' he said, indicating the grass between the verge and the Domecq bull. He took the gun from the glove-compartment and stuck it in his belt. 'I love you, Fran,' he said as he slammed the door.

He followed the course of the Jaguar until he lost it in the woods. He could still hear the sound of the exhaust. He climbed up the slope and lay flat on his back, staring up at the sky. Wisps of cloud floated in ever-changing shapes. The wound on his scalp was crusting. He took his fingers away and looked at them. No blood. It didn't even hurt too much any more. The chalet was six or seven miles away. Fran should be there by now. She was real class with more guts than most guys. Here was the courage that went with imagination. And the trouble was that she was never going to understand how he felt about her. It was no one's fault in particular. He'd been around for too long to find the right words for her, the courtly things that would make her happy. It had been a shitty thing to suggest that she wanted her money delivered by Brinks' van. God knows that they'd been happy with little enough. The itch to get more had been his alone.

It was half an hour before he heard the Jaguar again. He

ran down the slope to meet it. She pulled the convertible to the side and took off her sunglasses. They were on the sandy shoulder where the last of the fir-trees pushed down to the road.

'It's a chalet,' she said. 'Built of logs.'

'For God's sake,' he said impatiently. 'We *know* it's a goddam chalet!'

'In the middle of nowhere,' she went on composedly. 'Just cows and a couple of farms, nothing else. I drove straight on past and doubled back on the loop road.'

'Do you think that he noticed you?'

She nodded. 'You'd better believe it! He could hardly miss. He was putting the garage-doors up as I went by. He took a good long look at me.'

'Yeah, well, that does it,' he said. 'My first idea just isn't going to work. What's it like up there? Is there any sort of cover?'

'Trees,' she said. 'Pine-trees or something. There's a sort of plateau and they're all around it.'

He thought for a while. 'It isn't going to work,' he repeated. 'We were supposed to fly out tomorrow morning. Tyler's mind runs on tracks. He won't change his schedule. He'll have the chalet locked up like a fortress just as soon as night falls. No way is he going to open the door.'

'Well,' she said. 'It's a one-storey building sitting back off the road a bit. There's a kind of field behind, grass anyway, that I imagine belongs to the farm. And then all those trees, this creepy-looking wood.'

There was a constant churn of traffic along the lakeshore highway but it was quiet and peaceful where they were. De Wayne dragged the salt burn of tobacco deep into his lungs.

'Look, I know how this bastard thinks. He's got the bread and the bank's cool. The danger's over, he tells himself. But if someone comes knocking on his door after dark he's going to come alive remembering that he's sitting on a couple of million bucks.'

'So what happens?' she asked.

'We use guile,' he said. 'Out-psyche him! But first I need a look at the place. Turn the car around.'

She went into a three-point turn and headed the Jaguar back into the mountains. The road climbed in a series of S-bends, the silent strands of firs and pines sometimes above them and sometimes below. There was a flash of a red deer bounding across an open space. The air coming through the open windows was rarer and clearer.

'Coming up,' she said, nodding ahead. She pulled the car off the roadway into the trees. She cut the motor.

'There it is, to the right of the bus-shelter.'

He opened his door and walked to the edge of the trees to get a better look at the chalet. It was a couple of hundred yards along the road. He was looking at it sideways on. A farmhouse with a silo and outbuildings lay between the fringing trees and the chalet. Across on the other side of the road was a smaller farmhouse. He moved a few paces in the cool green shade. Iron piping fenced in a half-acre garden behind the chalet. Two of the windows were open but he could detect no sign of movement. He gauged the distance from where he was standing. Smoke was curling from the farmhouse chimney but the outbuildings were scattered in all directions. He ought to be able to make them, then use them as cover for the next break to the chalet. He walked back to the car.

'Do you see that barn?' He pointed and she nodded. 'Well, the moment you see me wave you get going. Drive straight to the chalet and ring the doorbell. OK, he hears it and peeks from the window. He's seen you before and now suddenly you're on his doorstep. His heart goes pitpat, right?'

'Right,' she said cautiously.

He went through the motions of opening a door and said, 'Yes?' He took Fran's part now. 'I'm Rod De Wayne's girlfriend and I want to know what you've done with him.'

Her iceberg eyes widened. ' "I want to know what you've done with him." You mean I actually say that?'

'That's what you say,' he said firmly. 'We'll assume that he's seen you outside the Seeturm Building. Now you've followed him here, OK? He's going to figure that I must have told you everything. So what does he do?'

She ran the tip of her tongue over her lips. 'That's simple and it's real jazzy. He drags me inside by my hair and shoots me. There's no one to hear and as soon as it's dark he gets rid of the Jaguar. Drowns it in the lake. The thing is, I'm not going anywhere near him.'

He leaned in through the lowered window and took her face in his hands. 'Will you listen to me, Fran? There won't *be* any shooting. He's going to be stalling for time. Trying to get you inside, sure. He's got to find out how much you know and whether anyone else knows as well. I wouldn't let you in there if there was any danger, Fran.'

She pulled away from his touch. 'You're making me hot and sticky.' She wiped her forehead and neck. 'It's good to hear that you'll be thinking about me. Where are you going to be while all this is going on?'

'Right behind you,' he said. 'That's why you've got to keep him talking at the door for as long as you can. I need to get the drop on him.'

'Jesus God,' she said. ' "*Get the drop on him!*" and you think this will work.'

'I *know* it'll work,' he promised. 'He'll probably hear the car. He's seen you in it before, alone. He runs to the window. His attention is on the front of the house not the back. Ten minutes at most and it'll be over, Fran. Two million dollars. *Trust* me, Fran. I can do it!'

She took a deep breath. 'You want me to go in with that "I'm Rod De Wayne's girlfriend" patter? You really mean it?'

Her obtuseness irritated him. He had a feeling that she was doing it purposely, putting it on.

'Ham it,' he said shortly. 'You've been playing those parts for half your life, it shouldn't be difficult. You haven't heard from me and you're desperate. That's why you've come here to find out what happened. The one big thing you've got going for you is that no way can he know I'm not dead. OK?'

131

She glanced up, her face suddenly serious. 'It's the last time, Rod. There isn't going to be any return performance.'

He shook his head. 'There'll be no need for one.' He took the gun, checked the clip and pumped a shell into the breech. Then he stuck the gun in his pocket and smiled at her. He moved away through the trees to the point nearest the out-buildings. The stretch of pastureland was unbroken by fences. There was nothing there but the herd of milk-cows, chomp-ing through the lush daisy-studded grass. He left the shelter of the trees and ran straight for the back of the barn. The line he had taken put him out of sight of the chalet. A bronze bell tinkled as the lead cow lifted her head. He jogged through the herd, followed by a cloud of biting cattleflies. The ground was soft from the April rains. Another fifty yards and he was safe in the shelter of the barn. This was built of wood with ventilation holes high in the walls. The doors were shut. He moved sideways, hands flat, inching in the direction of the farmyard. The heady smell of silage filled his nostrils. The concrete form of the manure-tank came into view, cats sleeping in the sunshine, hens scratching. Then a goose. He backed off hurriedly, remembering the aggressive habits of geese with strangers. When he reached the other end of the wall, he lifted his arm.

The Jaguar slid out from under the trees immediately. As it came on to the road, he broke for the back of the chalet. He ran hard with his head down, the gun ready in his hand. He was using the angles of the chalet to give him-self cover. There were fruit-trees in the garden, apple and pear. He vaulted the iron-piping fence and dashed through the fruit-trees. The car had stopped in front of the chalet. He tiptoed forwards to the back door. The handle turned under his grip as the front door-bell rang.

He opened and closed the door very quickly with his left hand, the gun in his right. The kitchen led off the hallway. The adjoining door was shut but he could hear Fran's voice.

'. . . last night when he didn't call me. Look, I *know* Rod. He just wouldn't do that, not without some very good reason. I want to know what that reason is!'

132

Then Tyler. 'What makes you think that I can help you?'

It sounded as if she were still standing on the doorstep and, as always when playing a part, convincing.

'There are a couple of things that you'd better get straight here. I flew to Europe a week after Rod did. And I *know* you can help me, Mister!'

De Wayne sank on his heels in front of the keyhole but the key was in the lock on the other side. The refrigerator whirred behind him. He straightened his back hurriedly.

'I see,' said Tyler. 'OK, I guess you'd better come in.'

De Wayne flattened himself behind the kitchen-door, staring down at the handle, the gun cocked. He heard the front door close, then there was nothing more for a few seconds. Carpet must be deadening the sound of their footsteps. Then Fran's voice came again, suddenly very clear.

'I'm sorry but I don't feel very well. I wonder if I might have a glass of water?'

Tyler sounded lazily confident. 'Sure. I'll get it for you.'

The door-handle revolved. The door opened inwards. Tyler's grip on it followed the forward movement, then relaxed, and the door swung freely. He had covered half the distance to the refrigerator when he was taken from behind, an arm around his throat, the barrel of De Wayne's gun digging into the side of his head. De Wayne spun him up against the wall. Tyler lifted his hands like a sleepwalker.

'Hi!' said De Wayne, grinning.

Shock wiped Tyler's face free of expression but fear stared from his eyes. The Brooks Brothers clothes and Racquets Club tie were as meaningless as the cheap cuckoo-clock over his head. He expected the worst quite plainly and was afraid.

De Wayne was enjoying every moment of it. 'Hi!' he said for the second time. 'You tried to kill me, you asshole!' he added cheerfully.

Tyler swallowed with difficulty. Then Fran appeared from the hallway, holding a twenty-two automatic in her hand.

'This was in the bedroom,' she said. 'The money's there too.'

The gun was a Belgian toy but lethal at close range. 'Get the Jag off the road,' said De Wayne. 'Out of sight somewhere. Put it in the garage. If there isn't room for the Volkswagen, too bad.'

She was looking the way she used to look in their days together at the Carmel Playhouse. Relaxed, poised and sure of her curtain-call. He winked at her and smiled.

'Ace, Fran. Just ace! Keep the gun and use it if you have to. Kent and I are going to have a little heart-to-heart about life in general. Right, Kent?'

Tyler spread his legs a little. He spoke without too much assurance. 'You won't kill me, Rod. You just know that you'd never make it without me.'

'Bullshit!' De Wayne's face lost its joviality. 'I'd kill you so fast, Kent! It would be like stamping on a roach. But it doesn't have to be like that. You see, what I'm going to do is take your money.'

The Jaguar started up outside. Tyler hung against the wall, crucified, staring at the top of De Wayne's head.

'I wish I'd blown your brains out,' he said bitterly.

De Wayne chuckled. 'You wish! That's the story of your life, Kent. No fucking follow-up. You're nothing but a phoney. Move!' He gestured towards the bedroom.

Tyler led the way down the corridor, his hands still high in the air. The bedroom was bleak. Worn carpet, varnished furniture, some sort of dried flowers in a glass case. Tyler's flight-ticket and the Mangan passport were on the dressing-table. The bag was on the bed.

'Open it up!' ordered De Wayne.

Tyler emptied the contents of the attaché-case. The bills dropped on to the counterpane.

'Count it!' said De Wayne.

Tyler assembled the bundles of bills, visibly worried still. De Wayne craned over the other man's shoulder, the gun now in Tyler's ribs. Then De Wayne's voice tightened in anger.

'Two hundred thousand? Don't give me that shit, Kent. I know how much there was to come, for Chrissakes! We've been on your tail all day. Where's the rest of it?'

He wrenched Tyler round and stuck the gun in the pit of his stomach. 'Just try me, Kent!' he whispered savagely. 'Try me, you bastard!'

Tyler's face had gone very pale. 'The rest is in bankers' drafts. They won't be ready until the morning.'

The front door opened and shut. Fran appeared carrying the twenty-two like a stage prop. She glanced from Tyler to De Wayne.

'What's the matter?' she asked quickly. 'What happened?'

De Wayne nodded at the pile of bills on the bed. 'That's all there is! Two hundred thousand! He says that he's collecting the rest in the morning.'

Fran stayed where she was in the doorway. 'But two hundred thousand dollars!' She dragged it out almost breathlessly. 'That's more than you ever dreamed of, Baby!'

Tyler had dropped his arms after the walk from the kitchen. De Wayne took a couple of paces backwards and glanced around the bedroom.

'He's lying,' he said contemptuously, coming back to Tyler. 'He's got it stashed somewhere.' The statement sounded wrong the moment he had made it. The iron bed and cheap furniture offered little scope for a hiding-place. 'For Chrissakes, Fran!' he barked suddenly. 'You're pointing that goddam thing straight at me!'

She swung the barrel hurriedly, aiming at Tyler. Her Slav features were hard in the afternoon sunshine.

'Why don't we just take whatever's there?' she begged. 'Think what we could do with it together, honey. If you love me, Rod, *do* it. *Please!*'

He shook his head obstinately. Tyler shifted his stance, his face sly as he looked at Fran.

'You're wasting your time,' he said. 'Sure, I tried to kill him but you haven't asked him why. And ask him about his other girlfriend while you're on the subject!'

His head rocked as the back of De Wayne's hand caught

him flush in the mouth. Tyler looked at the blood on his fingers and sneered through cut lips.

'Like it or not, Rod. You can't do without me.'

De Wayne swung round on Fran. His anger had turned to hatred and he was shaking.

'Can't you see what the bastard's trying to do? It's page one in the book, to turn you against me.'

'He's a killer, Fran,' Tyler said urgently. 'He killed a guy in the army. Threw him overboard after a poker-game.'

Fran caught De Wayne's arm as he lifted it to strike Tyler. 'Let's take the money and run,' she said. 'We can tie him up or something. That way there's nothing he can do about us.'

'No,' said De Wayne. He was standing in front of the window by the side of the bed. The clanking of the bell was drawing nearer. The dairy-herd crowded along the empty road outside, lowing softly as a boy in *lederhosen* drove them back to their barn. He was carrying a long peeled switch and accompanied by a crossbred German shepherd dog. He kept his eyes to the front as he passed the chalet.

'Sometimes I hate you for it,' Fran said quietly.

De Wayne looked at her as he had often looked at other people, couples especially, in search of whatever it was that had once held them together. In Fran it was easy to find. She loved him in a way that he could never match.

'Hell, no!' he said loudly, triggered by the slyness in Tyler's face. 'This bastard's going to suffer, Fran. One way or another he *has* to suffer!' He wrenched the closet-door open. 'In!' he said to Tyler.

Tyler hesitated. De Wayne grabbed a pillow from the bed and rammed his gun deep into the feathers.

'It's easy to kill you, you desperate fucker. Get in the goddam closet!'

Tyler stepped inside, the floor creaking under his weight. He was forced to bend his head and shoulders. De Wayne slammed the door and turned the key. Fran was still in the doorway.

'Let me ask you something,' he said. 'Have I ever failed you?'

She shook her head furiously, her eyes flooding. 'I'll never cry again, goddammit! What are you looking for, some sort of citation?'

'Trust and a little patience,' he answered. 'If he moves, use that closet as a shooting-gallery.'

He knew that she'd do no such thing but Tyler didn't. He ransacked one room after another, tearing out the few drawers and searching the commodes. There was nothing hidden that he could find, no evidence of Tyler's occupancy other than in the bedroom. He went out to the garage. Fran had switched the two cars around. The Volkswagen now stood on the small forecourt. He went through the glove-compartment and boot. Nothing there.

The sun was setting with April suddenness, the sombreness of the woods increasing. The pasture-land was empty of living things. There was neither man, bird nor beast. Smoke was coming from the second farmhouse. The whole scene was touched with a hint of haze and completely still. It was like the hush in a theatre just before the curtain rises. He lifted the garage-door. The building was fashioned from concrete blocks and there were no windows, no tool-chest, no more in the place than an old tyre hanging from a nail on the wall. He could see nothing that might be used to break or burrow out. He made his way back into the house through the kitchen. The garage door was secured by a stout tumbler lock. Fran was standing where he had left her, the gun dangling uselessly by her side. He took the weapon from her gently.

'I've got a long memory, honey and this is something that I have to do,' he said. 'It's either that or killing him.'

She lifted her shoulders despondently. 'I gave up a long time ago.'

But De Wayne's confidence had returned in a surging wave. 'He's telling the truth about the drafts. I'm sure of it. I'm going to go to the bank with him in the morning.'

'Then you're out of your mind!' Her eyes were fearful.

'He won't go through with it, Rod. Why should he? You'll be taking everything from him. He'll pull the plug on you, himself – everybody!'

'No,' he said, moving a finger from side to side. 'I'm going to make it worth his while. You'll see.'

Tyler had to be able to hear but it didn't seem to matter. De Wayne scooped the money back into the attaché-case and added the Mangan passport and the Swissair flight-ticket. He put the case on the bed and unlocked the clothes-closet. Tyler stumbled out, flexing his shoulders and neck. His face was red and his clothes rumpled.

De Wayne lifted his gun. 'OK, Kent. Here's what happens. I'm going to find a blanket or something for you and lock you in the garage. In the morning we'll go to the bank to-gether. Fran will stay here with your passport and the rest of the stuff.'

Tyler nodded warily. De Wayne grinned. 'You've got about twenty-four hours before all hell breaks loose. They're going to be coming at you from all angles, Kent. You know what I'm going to do? I'm going to give you the chance to run. You know, for old times' sake. A grand to keep you one jump ahead of the bloodhounds. How does that sound to you?'

Tyler shrugged. The fight had clearly left him. 'What in hell does it matter? It's too late for anything to matter.'

'You could just be right,' said De Wayne. 'For you it could be too late. But you'll run, old buddy. You'll run! Come on, let's get moving!'

TEN

IT WAS TEN MINUTES TO FOUR when Raven put his foot down, anchoring the Honda to the ground at the stoplights. The helmet the hire firm had supplied drowned out most of the noise but his body shook with the vibration of the engine. The *Balmoral* was a block away, an old-fashioned hotel up near the Zoological Gardens. He had checked in with Kirstie just before noon. The hall-porter had given him the name of the nearest garage that rented motor-cycles and Raven had gone straight out again. It was four years since he had ridden a machine but his driving-licence covered the operation. He spent the next three hours familiarising himself with the bike and exploring the city. Goggles and helmet made a perfect disguise and the Honda was capable of outgunning and outrunning a Porsche. On the other hand it could be wheeled up an alleyway at three miles an hour. It was the ideal cover for the job he was going to have to do.

The signals changed. He shot off up the hill and turned right on to a glistening strip of hardtop laid through lawns of Bermuda grass. The *Balmoral* was a Zürich institution and among other things the permanent home of several wealthy American matrons with nostalgic memories of the past. The terraced gardens were dotted with arbour-nooks, chairs and telescopes through which guests could survey the panorama of the lake beneath. A quarter-acre of glass protected floral hothouses. Signs printed in German, French and English

139

proclaimed tartly that GENTLEMEN WILL NOT PICK FLOWERS OTHERS MUST NOT.

Raven propped his machine near the entrance and snapped a chain through the spokes of the drive-wheel. He nodded to the doorman and walked into the lobby, carrying his helmet and goggles. The walls were hung with the stuffed heads of chamois and stylised engravings of cantonal scenes. A porter in leather jacket and striped apron was cleaning the brass for the second time that day. The sound of music came from the Palm Court. Raven crossed the lobby. A trio of middle-aged ladies, violin, cello and piano, were up on a dais near the vast French windows, rendering an extract from *Madame Butterfly*. The violinist led from her chair. The chink of china and the modulated tones of polite conversation formed a background to the string music. Most of the people taking tea were women, the exceptions being a youth with a goitre and an elderly man in a waistcoat with white piping who was leaning back in an armchair fast asleep.

Kirstie was sitting at a table by one of the French windows, cool in pale-green linen, her honey-hued hair tied behind her ears. He sat down, putting the goggles inside the helmet. There was a second cup and she filled it. He looked at the floating slice of lemon despondently. His taste in tea ran to the strong Indian leaf with plenty of sugar. He took a pastry filled with cream and raspberries.

'Did you manage to get any pictures?'

Her Nikon was on the table. He had suggested that she bring a camera, the idea being to get her mind off what he was doing. She ignored the question, adopting the air of faint surprise that she used when he had left the bath-water running or broken a plate.

'Do you realise that this is probably the stuffiest hotel east of Vancouver and you walk in here looking like a truck-driver?'

He glanced down and shrugged defensively. 'What's so wrong with me? The jeans are clean.'

She made a move of disapproval. 'Those filthy old sneakers

and the jacket's what's wrong. You're hardly inconspicuous. I mean, people are staring at you and you haven't even done anything yet! The whole thing is ridiculous – paying these outrageous prices so that you can meddle in somebody else's business.'

He lit a cigarette and leaned back, half-closing his eyes. The musical trio had moved on to Amy Woodford-Finden and *Pale Hands I Loved*.

'De Wayne's not in any hotel in the city. At least not under his right name. I had the hotel-porter check. But on the other hand, I had a good look at the bank.'

She poured herself more tea. 'You had a good look at the bank. Well, let me ask you something, Kamikaze Raven. Just what is that supposed to do for you?'

'Quite a lot,' he said mildly. 'The bank is my starting point.'

'You make me sick!' she said explosively. 'The last of the gang-busters!'

He kept his temper, glancing now at his watch. 'It's seven minutes to five, just over fourteen hours since you told me you wanted to come along. The understanding then was that there'd be no more criticism. OK, I didn't expect a Brunhild but I expected you to keep your promise.'

'Promise?' she said. 'I'm here because I worry about you, John. I worry when you're with me too but most of all when you're not. You've got me in such a state that I've been thinking of calling Jerry Soo.'

'Now that I wouldn't like,' said Raven. And then resentment took hold. 'Why the hell is it that I can never but *never* find a woman who understands me?'

'My God, you're naïve,' she answered. 'You don't *want* to be understood. What you want is someone who'll just go along with anything that you do or say.'

'Bullshit,' he said. 'Understanding isn't the same as approval. Look, Kirstie, I've done my best to explain. First of all it was Tyler and now it's the two of them. Nobody makes a clown of me, not without regretting it.'

She signed the bill and waited until the waitress had gone before answering.

'Look at yourself, my darling! You're thirty-nine years old with varicose veins and you're in somebody else's country. Small wonder that I thought about calling Jerry. You're out of control.'

'Chandler's taking the veins out in August,' he said doggedly. 'And Tyler picked the country. I may be thirty-nine years old but I'm nobody's patsy.'

She grabbed her camera and came to her feet, her face suddenly very flushed. 'I've tried looking at it the way you want me to. OK, I've helped you in the past. But this is different, John. These people are dangerous. They're killers.'

'People are looking at *you* now,' he said pointedly and lowered his voice. 'These guys are crooks and they're playing for high stakes. I intend to be the one to call them.'

She nibbled her lower lip, her eyes locking into his. 'There doesn't seem to be much future in any of this for me, does there, John? It hurts me to keep saying this but it's true. You don't need me. You don't need a woman. You don't need anyone.'

A quick feeling of fear returned, the fear of losing her. But he still couldn't bring himself to say the words that he knew she wanted to hear. She picked the room-key up from the table.

'Think about what I said, John. It matters very much to me.'

He spread his hands. 'You must know how I feel about you, Kirstie. I mean, come on now!'

'I think I do,' she replied pointedly. 'And I hope that I'm wrong.'

Heads turned as she made her exit from the room, her coltishness exaggerated by her anger. He collected his helmet and goggles and left them with the hall-porter. The man put them away under the counter.

'I used to ride a motor-cycle in London. Twice a day, to and from work, summer and winter.'

Raven smiled. 'At our age we're not looking to break

any speed records. But it's still the best way of seeing a city.'

The man leaned both elbows on the counter. 'I trained at the *Connaught*. Those were the days, sir.'

'Yes,' said Raven. 'They were indeed. What time do the banks open in the morning?'

'Eight o'clock. Reception will always help you.' He lowered his voice. 'But you get a better rate at the bank.'

Raven nodded. He went out into the garden. The arbour-seat he chose was wet with spray from the water-sprinkler. He wiped it off and sat down. The working day was nearing its end. The Zürchers finished early but then they started early too. The streets below were jammed with homebound traffic. Low-hanging mist obscured the surface of the lake. Tyler and De Wayne were out there somewhere, preparing for the score that would make monkeys out of the careful Swiss bankers. The concept was bold and imaginative. The more he thought about it, the surer he was of its success. All the elements were there. A skilled forger, a perfect front and, as far as Tyler was concerned, one-hundred-per-cent security. What fascinated Raven was how De Wayne would handle Tyler. The easy way out would be for Raven to pull the plug on both of them, have the police at the bank in the morning. But that would be meat without gravy. He liked it better the other way with Tyler and De Wayne each confident and he himself cast in the role of Nemesis.

This was no clean-run chase with the issue decided by bravery and endeavour. This was deception and treachery and because of it he wanted the partners to make their score and only then suffer. He looked at his watch. Six twenty. He went upstairs to the room to find Kirstie lying on the bed in her pants and bra. Her eyes were closed.

'I've been out in the garden, thinking,' he said.

She opened her eyes. 'I saw you from the window. And what was your decision?'

'About you and me, you mean?' He frowned and sat on the bed beside her. 'I didn't make a decision but I'll promise you something.'

She touched his greying hair with her fingertips. Her fine-skinned cheek was reddened where she had been lying on it.

'I won't believe a word of anything but I'll listen.'

He bent his head and kissed the mole above her navel. 'I'm going to be very very careful.'

She pulled his face up, looking down into his eyes. 'And that's it? This fabulous promise?'

'That's it,' he said, smiling.

They ate at seven o'clock and were out in the garden by eight. The lights had come on all over the city, tracing the boundary of the lake, glittering on the distant slopes. They sat for a while, holding hands and not talking. They were in bed and asleep before ten.

Raven awoke at seven with a familiar surge of excitement. He remembered the old days, the weeks of frustration with long waits on the end of a phone for the whispered voice that would tell him what he needed to know. This was the moment of truth.

He tiptoed from the bed to the bathroom, leaving the curtains drawn. Kirstie was still sleeping heavily, breathing through open mouth, one arm behind her head. He was quiet about washing and shaving. When he was dressed, he scribbled a note and left it propped against the telephone. Then he opened the drawer with care and slipped the thirty-eight into the pocket of his wind-cheater. The corridor outside was bright with early sunshine. Newly polished boots and shoes were lined up in front of the bedroom doors. The good smell of bacon and coffee made him feel hungry. He retrieved the goggles and helmet from the night-porter and made his way out into the clean morning air. The Honda one-two-five started under his thumb. Birds rose from the grass as the machine stuttered down the driveway. He found a café at the bottom of the hill and had his breakfast there, sitting among the neat and unspectacular men and women with their bourgeois virtues. And for that matter their bourgeois vices though his mind refused to carry him further. A quarter to eight saw him on Alfred-Escherstrasse with the places of business opening. He wheeled the Honda on to a parking-place for bikes and motor-cycles and sat there with his headgear on. It was a perfect position. There was only one entrance to the Credit-Union, obliquely across the street from the telephone-booths. He could see whoever came and went and was ready to sit there all day if necessary. Behind him was the arboretum and beyond that the lake.

The great bronze doors of the bank opened at eight precisely. The customers who had been waiting on the steps surged forward into the interior. Raven pushed up his goggles. He wiped the sweat from the bridge of his nose and his neck, still keeping his eyes on the bank-entrance. He ignored the cars that came and went. Eight-fourteen. Two men were climbing the steps. He recognised De Wayne first, still wearing the clothes he had worn in Paris, walking half a pace behind Tyler and moving with the deadliness of a stalking animal. It didn't look as if De Wayne was carrying a weapon although it was possible. Tyler had a case of some sort tucked under his left arm. Then both men were lost in the throng in the entrance-hall.

Raven dashed for the phone-booth. He dialled the *Balmoral Hotel* and gave his room number, never taking his eyes off the bank-entrance. Kirstie's sleepy voice came on the line.

'Hello?'

He imagined her tousled, the phone cradled in the pillow. 'It's me,' he said quickly. 'Look, there's no time for long explanations. De Wayne and Tyler have just gone into the bank. When they come out I'm going to follow them.'

There was no answer and for a moment he thought that she had hung up on him. His voice was sharp.

'Kirstie? What is it?'

'I heard,' she replied. 'Let me ask you one question, John. Have you taken that gun with you?'

The weight in his pocket was suddenly heavy. 'Yes,' he answered. The line went dead. This time there was no question about it. She'd slammed the phone down on him. He left the booth replacing his goggles and took his seat on the Honda again. The map of the city and canton of Zürich was open on top of the gas-tank. They knew where they were going. He didn't. It was the only edge they had on him now. Trams rumbled in the distance. His anti-glare goggles tinged everything yellow, even the trees and the grass. He continued to watch the steps to the bank thinking about Kirstie. He owed it to her to keep his promise. But then he'd been making the same promise to someone or other all his life, beginning with his sister. Things would always work out if only they'd leave him alone.

De Wayne and Tyler were out in ten minutes. A significant change had taken place. This time it was De Wayne who was carrying the attaché-case. He glanced right and left before giving Tyler the signal to cross the street. There was no question who was calling the shots. De Wayne kept what looked like a friendly grasp on Tyler's sleeve but Raven was under no illusion. The couple walked to a Volkswagen that was parked thirty yards away. Raven dropped his machine from the rest and pressed the starting button. The Volkswagen pulled out from the kerb, Tyler at the wheel. Raven stayed well behind, content to get the odd glimpse of the hunched vehicle, the open map wedged beneath the strap around the fuel-tank. The Volkswagen led him south on Alfred-Escherstrasse, past the cut-off that led to the Luzern highway and on to the lakeshore motor-road. It was easier now to follow his quarry. He had the registration number of the vehicle in his head, traffic was heavy and the few turn-offs were on one side of the highway.

It was almost nine o'clock with the sun beginning to generate heat. Pleasure-craft were out on the ruffled water. Handsome villas stood serene on the wooded hillsides. A girls' school offered a glimpse of nubile tennis-players. Raven pulled out suddenly and accelerated past a dozen vehicles. The Volkswagen was nowhere in sight. He increased his speed, passing a line of cars, but there was no sign of the one he was meant to be following. Tyler must have turned off somewhere. One of the villas, perhaps. Even the girls' school. He swung into an illegal U-turn, braving the indignation of other drivers, and hustled back scanning the opposite side of the highway. And then he saw it, the cut-off hidden by trees. Emtal and Birnenberg. A graphic sign warned of falling rocks and ice in winter. He waited for a lull in the traffic and then wheeled across to the cut-off. A Domecq bull dominated the hillside. The mountain road was gouged deep into it.

Raven leaned into the curve, gunning his motor. The pine-trees blurred above his head. He was hitting a hundred and twenty kilometres an hour, the fastest he had ever gone on two wheels. He held this speed until his ears detected the drone of a car in front of him. The road turned and twisted and he could see nothing. But instinct told him that it was the Volkswagen ahead. He throttled down, gauging his speed to bring the car into view. It was another mile before he had his first glimpse. The Volkswagen was climbing steadily, hugging the bank. There was no soft shoulder. Raven dropped back quickly. The camber of the road changed abruptly. The fir-trees were wider spaced, the plantation was dark and silent in spite of the sunshine. Then suddenly he saw the sky again, vast and blue above the lush pastureland. The plateau appeared to be about two miles long by one wide and edged with fir-trees. He could see herds of cows meandering over the grass. The only signs of human habitation were a couple of farmhouses and a chalet. The Volkswagen turned in beside it.

Raven killed his motor and watched the two men walk across from the garage. The front door opened and they disappeared from view inside. He glanced down at his map. The village of Birnenberg was eight hundred feet higher up. He could just see the huddle of houses against white rock under a snow-capped peak. A loop joined the far end of the plateau to the mountain road a few miles from the lake. He wheeled the Honda into the trees, propped it up and took off his helmet and goggles. He lit a cigarette and gazed across the grass. The telephone-poles followed the road. Wires linked with the chalet and farmhouses. There was only one way out for De Wayne and Tyler. And as long he he could get to a phone he could block it. But that wasn't for now. There was a lot to be done before then. He took the gun from his pocket and checked the three rounds that remained in the chambers.

ELEVEN

KIRSTIE HAD STARTED TO CRY long before she put the tele-phone down, in fact the moment she had noticed the half-open drawer. She buried her head in the pillows despairingly. He had no *right* to do this to her! She'd been alone for so long until he appeared in her life. Everyone else had gone. Her father first and then her brother Jamie. The year with Raven had not been easy. She had soon realised that there was no question of marriage. He had never known about her visit to the *Clinique Morel*, the misery of lying behind drawn curtains in daylight and thinking about the child she could now never have. God damn Raven! *God damn him!*

She sat up in bed, wiping her eyes with the top of the sheet. He should never have left the police-force except that even there he had been a loner. The only guy in step. Part-time friend and part-time lover, part-time everything. The only thing in his world that claimed his complete attention was this obsession with the chase. It was like a disease, this need to involve himself with criminals and then hunt them down. Like some sort of bounty-hunter who never claimed his reward.

Why *him* of all people! Her exasperation grew. If only she'd known what he was really like at the beginning. She shook her head miserably. That wouldn't have worked either. She would still have gone the same route. The real problem was that she loved him. Period. Her watch was on the bed-side table. It was twenty minutes past eight. She reached

149

for the telephone. She knew the number by heart. The Soos were the only real friends that she had left. She had to talk to *someone*. John was no longer making sense. She couldn't just *sit* there waiting for some dreadful news. The call clicked through the circuits, each electronic impulse bringing her closer to the apartment overlooking the Thames. Jerry would surely give her the help that she needed. John was his friend and he knew the pig-headed stubbornness that was at the root of this crazy behaviour. Jerry would be able to tell her the right thing to do. The number continued to ring and rang for five minutes before she gave up. Louise could be anywhere, out shopping or even on a concert-tour. Jerry was probably on his way to work. If he hadn't yet arrived she could leave a message for him to call her back. In the meantime she would shower and dress. Anything was better than just lying there worrying.

She dialled Jerry Soo's outside line at New Scotland Yard. A completely strange voice answered.

'Six-two-six-two. Detective-Sergeant Baxter speaking.'

'I'd like to talk with Detective-Inspector Soo, please. It's a personal matter. If he hasn't yet arrived you could ask him to call me back. I'll give you my number.' She read it from the disc on the telephone rest.

The man's voice was regretful. 'Detective-Inspector Soo's in Hong Kong, I'm afraid. He won't be back for a week. Is there any way that I could help?'

'No.' She shook her head. 'No, it doesn't matter.' But it did and she put down the phone with a presentiment of danger. Something terrible was about to happen and there was no one to help her. No one at all. She was out of the bathroom and dressed by nine o'clock. She stuffed her passport and money in her bag and stared at herself in the full-length mirror. There was no sign of the turmoil she was enduring, the fear and the cry for help. Nothing more than a lady in a Stephen Lloyd spring dress wearing a little too much make-up. It had come to be a habit over the past twelve months like chilli-con-carne, cold beer and Brahms. All the things he liked and required her to share. She rang the desk for a cab. It was waiting outside by the time she went down. She leaned back as the driver turned his head.

'Police-headquarters,' she said. 'The criminal police.'

They dropped four hundred feet with the stop-lights in their favour all the way down. The driver braked outside a stone building between the Rathaus and Bahnhofstrasse. He jerked his head sideways.

'*Krimipolizei!*'

She paid him off and went inside. Sunshine seemed to follow her, filling the entrance-hall and corridors with a limpid searching light. She answered the uniformed police-man who approached in French.

'Could I see someone who speaks English, please, Monsieur?'

'*Un moment, Madame.*' The man had the guttural delivery of the Swiss-German using his second language. He reappeared with a younger man in plain clothes. His English had clearly been learned from books.

'Good morning, Madame. What do you wish?'

The uniformed cop had moved out of earshot but people were coming and going. She lowered her voice.

'I want to report a crime. Two and a half million dollars' worth of forged bearer-bonds have just been cashed at the Laudesbank on Alfred-Escherstrasse.'

The plain-clothes man had leather cuff-links and smelled pleasantly of soap. He looked at Kirstie sharply as she swayed.

'Are you not well, Madame?'

She shook her head. 'Perhaps – if I might have a glass of water.' She hadn't eaten or drunk since the previous evening.

The man brought her a plastic cup. The water was flat and tasteless. She was suddenly conscious that people were peeking at her from doorways. The plain-clothes man took the empty cup.

'If you will come, please!'

She followed him down a bright airy corridor, green with

house plants. He tapped on a door, went through and was out again almost immediately.

'Please!' he said, smiling politely and holding the door open for her. The room she entered overlooked the river. She could see the pleasure-craft moored to the stakes below and covered with tarpaulin sheets. The door closed discreetly. The man she was left with was tall and wide-shouldered. He was dressed in a soft tweed suit and wore spectacles and a Polka-dotted bowtie. He reminded her of the tennis pro at the Racing Club. Both men had the same easy smile and manner that generated confidence. He offered a chair and held out his hand.

'Criminal-Commissioner Städelmann. *Polizeüinspektorat.*'

'I'm Kirstie Macfarlane.' His handshake was light but firm.

'Sit down, Mrs Macfarlane.'

This was a much sounder command of the English language with a hint of Oxford in the vowel sounds.

'That's Miss,' she corrected and crossed her legs.

Städelmann raised sandy eyebrows, proffering the box of cigarettes on his desk. She took one, leaning into the flame of the match that he held. The tobacco was Egyptian.

'Do you know the expression "a paperhanger", Mr Städelmann?'

He nodded. 'A forger. There is something similar in German.'

'Well, that's what you're dealing with,' she said and looked him straight in the eye. 'Paperhangers who have unloaded two and a half million dollars' worth of forged bearer-bonds. Right here in your city. And a man's life is in desperate danger.'

Städelmann held up a hand, his expression serious. He reached over the desk and switched on a tape-recorder. The openness of his manoeuvre made a colleague of her rather than a suspect.

'Tell me everything,' he said quietly.

She found herself pouring it all out, beginning with the photographic session in the Bois de Boulogne. Städelmann listened in silence, his look flicking from Kirstie's face to the tape revolving in the recording-machine.

'I'm scared,' Kirstie said at the end. '*Scared*, do you understand? Not for myself. There's something you have to realise about this man, Mr Städelmann. He doesn't think the way ordinary people do. It isn't just that he's mule-headed. He's got a strong impression that he's God.' She tried to smile and failed. Städelmann pressed a button. The plain-clothes man who had escorted Kirstie appeared in the doorway.

'*Zu!*' barked Städelmann. The detective stepped inside and shut the door.

Städelmann extended his hand. 'You have your papers, Miss Macfarlane?' She took her passport out of her bag and gave it to him. Städelmann glanced through the document and added to the notes he had already made.

'And your hotel here in Zürich?'

'The *Balmoral*,' Kirstie replied.

Städelmann handed his papers to his subordinate and spoke in German. The man opened the door and left them alone again.

'Mr Raven is your sweetheart?' He used the old-fashioned term without a trace of self-consciousness.

She raised her eyes. 'Yes. You could say my common-law husband.'

'Ah!' He considered her shrewdly. 'Let me be frank, Miss Macfarlane. I find a lot of what you have told me very difficult to accept. Especially the motives of your friend.'

The pattern of sunlight had moved across the wall since she had entered the room. She opened the box and took another of Städelmann's cigarettes. He lit it for her courteously. She inhaled deeply.

'I've done my best to explain. It isn't easy.'

'Why didn't you go to the police in the first place?' he asked gently.

She let the tobacco-smoke go with a sigh. So much seemed to have happened in so short a time. If she had gone to the police right at the beginning, before John had come over from London, things might have been different. But she hadn't and once John had taken control the choice was no longer hers. *This* was what she couldn't make them understand. The way she had to give in, step by step, hoping that each time would be the last.

'I wanted to talk to John. He was still in London.'

'But he came to Paris,' Städelmann said mildly.

'You don't understand,' she said desperately. 'John *wanted* to go to the police in the first place. I was the one who objected.' She told him about Suzini.

Städelmann made no comment about the visit to the commissariat. 'If what you say is true the bank will be paying out a very big reward. Is it possible that this is what Mr Raven is after?'

She moved her head from side to side. 'No. He doesn't care about money, not in that sort of way. And in any case he has more than enough to live comfortably.'

Städelmann stared out through the window. Suddenly he turned towards her. 'I'll be frank with you, Miss Macfarlane. The more I hear about Mr Raven, the less I approve of him. The one positive fact we seem to have established is that he is an ex-detective with a total contempt for the law.'

'That just isn't right,' she argued. 'You've got it all wrong. It isn't the *concept* of law that he fights, it's the people who administer it. The clue is somewhere in there. *This* is his real problem. He wants to be the cop, the judge and the jury. Can't you understand? I don't suppose he's done a single thing in his whole life that he thinks of as being dishonest.'

'It becomes worse and worse,' Städelmann said sombrely. Somebody knocked on the door. High-power communications had produced a sheaf of papers that the younger detective placed on Städelmann's desk. He took a position against the wall near the windows, avoiding Kirstie's look. The Commissioner glanced through the papers quickly, taking his time with the telexed messages. The tape was still turning on the recording-machine. He raised his head and looked at Kirstie.

154

'Laudesbank have not dealt in General Chemical securities of any kind since January this year. That's number one. Number two : They do not know anyone called Kent Tyler, nor have they heard of Rod De Wayne.'

She felt the blood surging to her neck and face. 'There has to be some kind of mistake. I mean, I *know* I'm right! Look, a man's life is in danger. Don't you believe me?'

'I haven't finished,' said Städelmann. 'The bank paid out two million dollars in cash and letters-of-credit to one man yesterday. Someone called Petersen. Now he just might be Tyler. Think carefully, have you ever heard of a company called Chase Mutual?'

She shook her head impatiently. 'Never! Look, can't you *understand*, Mr Städelmann — John Raven's following these men and they'll kill him!'

He ignored the question, looking down at one of the telex messages. 'I have a request here from the French police, Miss Macfarlane. They ask for your detention and the detention of Mr John Raven.'

'But that's absurd!' Her mouth was suddenly dry. She closed her eyes. The next thing she knew she was standing in front of the open window, supported by Städelmann. His jacket was soft and smelled of lavender-water. The young detective gave her another glass of water. She drank it, wiped her forehead and sat down.

'I'm sorry. I don't usually do that sort of thing.' It was true and this was the last place she would have chosen to do it. 'You used the word "detention". Does that mean arrested? What am I supposed to have done? I came here voluntarily.'

His eyes were shrewd. 'This is a request for detention pending enquiries. The remains of a man have been discovered near Sully-la-Forêt. A car registered in your name was seen in the town and it seems that Mr Raven was making enquiries about the house where the man was killed.'

'But I've explained all that,' she burst out. 'I want to know where John is!'

She wanted to believe in Städelmann but remembered

the tales that Raven had told her, the tricks that detectives used to instil confidence in their victims.

Städelmann consulted his watch. 'I'm afraid we don't know where *anyone* is at the moment. But what we *can* do is make sure that none of these gentlemen leaves Switzerland. We might find out more in a moment. Detectives are at the offices of Chase Mutual. It appears that another bank is involved. In the meantime three men have vanished into thin air. Where did Mr Raven hire his motor-cycle?'

She tried to think. 'I can't remember. No, wait a minute! I'm almost sure he said something about getting the name of the hire-firm from the doorman at the hotel. Maybe that would help?'

Städelmann used the telephone, speaking again in German. He replaced the instrument. His voice and manner were sympathetic.

'I can arrange for you to stay here for a while if you like. There are girls in the building who speak English. You would be near at hand.'

She shook her head. 'If I'm free, then I want to go back to the hotel. John may try to get in touch with me. If I'm not free, I would like to see a lawyer.'

Städelmann stopped the recording-machine. 'You're free.' he said quietly. 'But I shall have to ask for your passport.'

She gave it to him. 'Can you tell me the name of the Canadian Consul?'

'Of course!' He glanced across at the younger detective. 'Mr Lauterbach will drive you there.'

She came to her feet, needing his help yet unsure of it. 'You have been very kind, Commissioner. I just wish I could make you understand.'

He smiled and gave her his hand. 'I think I do, Miss Macfarlane. Now see your Consul, then go back to the hotel. As soon as there is news I will let you know. Lauterbach!'

The younger detective's heels came together. 'Commissioner!'

'Take Miss Macfarlane wherever she wants to go.'

*

Lauterbach escorted her to the compound at the rear of the building. He opened the rear door of a black BMW, handed her into the car and took the wheel.

'Where may I drive you, please?' His courtesy was tinged with embarrassment.

She could see his face in the driving mirror. He was staring straight ahead.

'The Canadian Consulate, please,' she said.

A uniformed officer held the traffic so that the BMW could emerge. It was a pleasant drive along the north shore of the lake. The need for reassurance was strong and she tried to talk a couple of times. But Lauterbach refused to be drawn, answering only in monosyllables. He was clearly torn between the necessity to observe correct behaviour and the danger of fraternisation. He turned the BMW between gates and past grass that was verdant under spring sunshine. Lauterbach braked stylishly and was out in time to open the door for her.

'I shall wait, Miss,' he announced awkwardly.

'Thank you,' she said. His face reddened.

A middle-aged man in a hard-wearing grey suit was sitting at a desk in the hallway. There was a coloured photograph of the Queen hanging on the wall, a Maple-Leaf flag and the usual obligatory notices both in French and in English. The man at the desk wore a row of campaign ribbons and had a strong Nova Scotian accent. He took her name and showed her into a waiting-room. There was a distant view of the lake, more notices and a ticker-tape machine. A couple of yards of unread agency-reports trailed across the carpet. She glanced through them quickly, half-expecting to read Raven's name or even her own, but there was nothing. The minutes lengthened to twenty before the Nova Scotian reappeared.

'Will you come this way, Miss Macfarlane?'

He accompanied her to a room on the second floor, knocked and announced her.

'Miss Macfarlane, sir!'

A sun-tanned six-footer came towards her behind outstretched hand, 'Hi! How are you? Bill Sanders, Vice-Consul. Now what can I do for you?'

He dressed in keeping with the outdoor look. Seersucker suit, white loafers and button-down collar. There was a better view of the lake, comfortable chairs and a couple of waist-high urns in which lemon-trees were growing. She took out a cigarette and lit it. Her fingers were shaking and she would probably throw up but she had to go through with it.

Sanders tilted a leg over his knee and admired his silk sock. 'What seems to be the trouble, Miss Macfarlane?'

It was all there in the voice, United Empire Loyalists, Ridley College and probably one of the better American universities. She raised her eyes.

'It's the police.'

The word brought him up straight. 'How do you mean, the police?'

She put her cigarette down and locked the fingers of her hands together to stop them from trembling. The vibes she was getting from Sanders were anything but sympathetic. She recounted her story for the second time, a shorter and edited version that Sanders heard out with growing displeasure.

'Now let me get this straight,' he said weightily. 'This man you are travelling with is a British subject who is wanted by both the French and Swiss police?' He managed to make it sound an affront to his office.

'That's hardly the point,' she said steadily.

'Then just what *is* the point?' replied Sanders. 'Look, I'm sorry if you've got yourself into a jam. But I don't really see what I can do for you. You're obviously not in police custody and this guy will have to take care of himself. We're not running a Lonely Hearts Bureau here, you know.'

'Maybe not,' she said, coming to her feet, her face flaming. 'But then nor are you running a helpful consular service! A grizzly bear would have shown more understanding than you have. Remember that when you answer the letter!'

Sanders blinked pale eyelashes, clearly surprised by her outburst. 'What letter is that, Miss Macfarlane?'

'The one I send to Ottawa,' she answered. She went out, slamming the door, and felt better for it. She passed the Nova Scotian without giving him a look or word. The back of the BMW was suddenly a friendly place. Lauterbach turned his head.

'What directions now, please?'

'The *Balmoral Hotel*,' she said. Neither of them spoke on the journey there. The BMW was unmarked, and Lauterbach in plain clothes, but she felt the change of atmosphere as she crossed the lobby to Reception. The desk clerk gave her the room-key. The two French windows opening on to the balcony were wide, a couple of resident American matrons on their chaise-longues there were visibly interested in what was going on inside. The clerk lowered his voice discreetly.

'The police have been here, Madame. They insisted on visiting your room.'

'Thank you,' she answered, clutching her room-key firmly. 'Visiting' was a euphemism for 'searching'. She would probably be asked to leave the hotel. She ran the gauntlet of curious looks as far as the lift and rode up to her room. She closed the door behind her and stood with her back against it. Her room had been methodically searched without any attempt to hide the manoeuvre. Clothes had been replaced in drawers that were left half-open. The papers relating to Raven's rented motor-cycle had disappeared.

She did her best to remember whether or not Raven had taken his passport with him. It suddenly seemed important. She hung a DO NOT DISTURB sign outside the door, and drew the curtains and lay down on the bed. She must have slept. The phone startled her into instant awareness and she snatched at the instrument.

'Hello?'

It was Städelmann. 'I would like you to come down here again if that is possible, Miss Macfarlane.' His voice sounded avuncular but she was no longer sure about anyone.

'Yes,' she said hesitantly. 'Yes, of course.'

A cab took her downtown again. It was just after five

and people were leaving police headquarters. The ubiquitous Lauterbach picked her up at the entrance and took her to Städelmann's office. The Commissioner greeted her kindly. The avuncular manner had not slipped.

'I just had a word with your vice-consul. I assured him that there was no question of your arrest. At least, not for the moment.'

'For the moment,' she repeated blankly. Surely he hadn't brought her all the way down here just to tell her that. She was sitting quite close to his desk. For a moment she had a strange feeling that he was about to take her hand. But all he did was smile.

'I said I would let you know if there was news.'

She nodded. 'They searched my room.'

He dismissed the thought with well-manicured fingers. 'A formality. We needed the Honda papers.'

She drew a long breath. 'Is there any news of John?'

He nodded, still smiling. 'Mr Raven made an illegal U-turn at nine-seventeen this morning near Budelheim. A public-spirited citizen took his number and informed the traffic-police.'

She blinked. 'What does that mean?'

Städelmann spread his hands. 'It means that now we have his description. It won't be long before we trace him. There is something else. Petersen *is* Tyler. The bonds were not deposited with Laudesbank. They were used as collateral with another bank in Zürich. Then the money borrowed was transferred to the account of Chase Mutual. The secretary there has been of great assistance. So, you see, it all begins to fit together.'

'Of course,' she said quickly. 'That's what I told you.'

Städelmann glanced at the clock. 'We have been in touch with General Chemical. The corporate secretary is taking the first flight out.'

She wet her lips now, sick from hunger. 'So what do we do?'

This time he did pat her hand. 'We wait,' he said comfortably. 'One thing is sure. No one is leaving Switzerland.'

TWELVE

TYLER TURNED THE IGNITION-KEY, stilling the clatter of the Volkswagen. The plateau was quiet in the morning sunshine. There was a strange peace about the scene, the slow-moving cows hock-deep in meadow-grass, woodsmoke corkscrewing up into a cloudless sky. And around it all the fringe of dark-green firs. Tyler raised his head. The two men stared at one another.

De Wayne had the bag with the bank-papers in his lap. The gun was in his hand. He was completely relaxed. He smiled, using Tyler's army nickname.

'How's it feel, Dasher?'

Tyler made no answer.

'An asshole,' De Wayne said comfortably. 'That's what you are, Kent. An incompetent asshole.'

Tyler showed no expression. He had acted like a zombie ever since they had left the bank, obeying instructions stone-faced, without opening his mouth. Like a man at the end of his tether. The thought afforded De Wayne a great deal of satisfaction. He glanced right and then left along the empty stretch of road. Snowcapped peaks soared in the far distance. There was no sign of life in either of the two farmhouses. De Wayne opened the door on his side.

'Out!'

Fran met them in the hallway. She looked from De Wayne's face to the bag that he was carrying. He winked, smiling back at her.

161

'It worked like a dream. We just made a major withdrawal.'

Relief flooded into her face. For his safe return or the loot? He wasn't sure but then Fran had to have the benefit of the doubt. So it was probably the money. Known form went by the board when two million dollars were involved. They were in the kitchen now with nothing in view beyond the window but the end of the barn, the fir-trees and inevitable mountains. De Wayne put the bag on top of the refrigerator and indicated a chair with the gun.

'Sit down, Dasher, and keep your hands on top of the table. That's right, up where I can see them!'

Tyler obeyed, dragging out each movement but complying. His suit was creased after the night in the garage. His face had aged ten years since the previous night. He sat, staring at his well-kept fingernails, his head slightly bowed. Fran was standing just inside the doorway.

'Get the stuff from the bedroom, hon,' said De Wayne. 'All of it. The passport and flight-ticket.'

'You want the money too?'

'Ah yes,' he said quickly. 'Everything.' They could have been back in Carmel, she was so cool. Sitting in the old Mustang convertible with the top down, indifferent to tourists and the Valley gentlemen-ranchers alike. It was the way he liked her best. Desirable, slightly contemptuous of other men and, more than anything else, his woman.

She carried the things in, placed them on the kitchen-table and came to his side.

'Now,' he said, widening his stance. 'Let's see what we have here. Two million bucks in certified deposits. That means whoever has 'em gets paid, honey. And then there's the cash money.'

'Stop being a ham,' Fran said quietly. 'You're making a fool of yourself.'

'You think?' He cocked his head on one side, showing all his teeth.

'I *know*,' she retorted. 'Don't be so goddam sure of yourself. There's one thing that you seem to have forgotten.'

'What's that?'

'The girl's boyfriend, the ex-cop. He's probably here by now.'

'So what?' De Wayne answered equably. Every word that they spoke dragged Tyler with them one way or another and yet he might have been a log of wood. 'You and I are still in Paris as far as Raven's concerned. He's got the wrong bank and he's a day late.'

A thrush alighted on the window-sill outside, flying away again as it caught sight of them. De Wayne tossed the Irish passport across the table. He followed it with the flight-ticket and then counted out ten hundred-dollar bills. He tucked these under the other two documents. The stuttering of a motor-cycle sounded across the plateau.

De Wayne grinned behind his gun. 'Nothing's ever going to be the same for either of us, Kent. Never.'

Tyler had made no move to touch any of the articles on the table in front of him.

'Pick 'em up, Kent,' said De Wayne. 'Stick 'em in your pocket. That's your survival-kit!'

Tyler's movements were very slow. He paused for some time, looking at the bills in his hand.

'Now let me explain the facts of life,' De Wayne said cheerfully. The noise of the motor-cycle was no longer to be heard. 'You outsmarted yourself, old buddy. And look what happened! You can't afford to go to the law. You've shown your face all over this town. *And* you fronted the bank. What would you tell them, Kent? That the bonds were forged and your old friend clipped you?'

A hornet buzzed uselessly in a spider's-web on the window-pane. Tyler's face was set in hatred. There was sweat on his forehead.

'I wish to God I *had* killed you,' he said bitterly.

'You bet!' De Wayne's grin grew wider. 'But you always were a lousy shot. No, Kent. You've been taken to the cleaners and there's not a goddam thing that you can do about it except get in your car and take a long hike. The grand is just for old times' sake. You're worth more to me alive than dead. That way at least I can be sure that you're going to remember. And you will remember, won't you, Dasher?'

The muscles in Tyler's face tightened. He moved very quickly for a big man, tipping the table from below. The edge caught De Wayne in the stomach, sending him sideways as he lurched forward. He heard Fran's scream as Tyler's hand knocked her over and then Tyler was airborne. De Wayne fired twice in rapid succession. Both shells took Tyler in the chest. He seemed to hang in the air, an enormous bubble of bright-red blood appearing in his open mouth. He was dead before he hit the floor. He lay on his face, the pool of blood spreading beneath him. The chalet rang with the echo of the double explosion.

De Wayne picked himself up and shoved Fran into the living-room. He yanked the phone-cord out of the wall.

'Get the goddam car out!' he ordered. Fran was standing against the wall with her fingers covering her mouth. '*Move!*' he said and ran to the window. There was no sign of alarm that he could see. He took a second look at the front of the chalet. The empty road stretched invitingly. There was no indication that the shots had been heard. Fran had the Jaguar out with the motor running. The Volkswagen was parked on the highway. Fear, curiosity, something that was stronger than judgement, drew him back into the kitchen. Tyler's hair was white against the dark floor. Flies had landed near the viscous pool. The room stank of death but De Wayne had a strange feeling of defeat, as though the other man in death had achieved some kind of victory.

He locked the back door and went out through the front of the chalet. He chucked the bags in the back of the convertible. Fran was behind the steering-wheel, wearing dark glasses. It was impossible to know what was going on behind them. He climbed in beside her.

'I had to do it, Fran, honey,' he pleaded. His voice sounded rusty as though it hadn't been used in years. 'Goddammit, you *saw* what happened!'

She turned her head, raising the sun-glasses as if to get a

clearer view of him. Her face revealed the emotions he had always guessed at but never actually seen in her. Compassion, resignation and loyalty. She would never turn her back on him or desert him, above all not now.

'We can be in Germany in less than an hour,' he said quietly. She nodded. He touched her hand hesitantly. 'Then we'd better get going!'

'But which *way*?'

He gestured nervously with his right hand. The fingers stank of burnt cordite. He locked the gun in the glove-compartment and consulted the Hallweg road-atlas.

Fran turned her head as he looked up. 'What is it, honey? What's troubling you?'

He fished behind the seat, feeling for the bag that contained the money and the bank-papers.

'The phone,' he said. 'Yanking it out of the wall like that. Why did I do it? *He's* sure as hell not going to use it.'

'That's right,' she said quickly and put her hand on his knee. 'Snap out of it, baby. It's over and there's nothing that anyone can do about it. He's dead.'

He nodded. 'He had it coming, Fran. You were there and you saw. *You* know he had it coming.'

He might have been a child, stumbling into the house with a cooked-up story that he already knew was doomed. But she played the rules to save both of them, soothing, holding and protecting.

'We have to go,' she said in a matter-of-fact voice.

He pulled himself together with an effort and looked down at the road-atlas again. 'Forget Germany! We'll do what we planned in the first place, double back into France. We'll take the first plane out of Paris. It's beautiful, Fran. Don't you see it? It's going to be a long time before anyone goes in there.' He nodded across at the chalet.

'There's a woman watching us,' Fran said without turning her head. 'She's standing in the doorway of the farmhouse.'

He flattened himself in his seat, looking up into the rearview mirror. The woman was a couple of hundred yards away. It was too distant for him to determine her features.

'She couldn't have seen or heard anything,' he said defensively. It was a prayer rather than a statement. The woman vanished even as he watched. Smoke curled from the farmhouse chimney. The track between there and the highway was empty. 'Sure,' he said, heartened. 'Those shots could have come from anywhere.'

Fran didn't answer. He glanced sideways and saw the tears in her eyes. 'For fuck's sake, Fran,' he pleaded. 'Don't *do* this to me!'

She shook her head, brushing at her eyes. 'It isn't me. It isn't you. Nobody's doing anything to anybody! It's just the way things are. I'd rather not talk, Rod. I don't know what to say any more.'

'Sure,' he said sadly. 'There's nothing to say in any case. Move over and let me take the wheel. It'll be better for both of us.'

He got out of the car and they exchanged places. It was odd to think that he had wanted Tyler alive and had ended by killing him. He felt no remorse, no more regret that an ace manoeuvre had been placed in jeopardy.

'Put your seat-belt on,' he said mechanically and buckled his own strap. He put the Jaguar in low gear and pressed on the accelerator. The plateau dropped away above them.

They had travelled a hundred yards when he suddenly put his foot on the brake and switched off the ignition. He stuck his head through the open window then turned to face Fran. The stutter of an engine was growing fainter.

'A motor-bike,' she said hesitantly.

'God*dammit*, Fran!' he snarled. 'I *know* it's a motor-bike!'

He switched on again and slammed into reverse. He backed as far as a knoll that offered a view through the trees and across the plateau. He scrambled up the bank with Fran close behind. Their eyes followed the helmeted motor-cyclist until he dismounted in front of the chalet. It was quiet where they were among the pine-trees and he could hear Fran's unhurried breathing. He held her wrist tightly as they watched the newcomer try first the front door and then the windows. There was nobody else in sight. Even the animals were hidden. The only sign of life was the curl of smoke from one of the farmhouse chimneys. The motor-cyclist removed his goggles and helmet. He was almost a quarter of a mile away but there was no doubt at all about his identity.

De Wayne cleared his throat huskily. 'I don't *believe* it! It's that bastard Raven!'

He swung round, slithering and slipping in his hurry to get back to the car. He ploughed down the bank, sand filling his shoes. Fran caught up with him as he unlocked the glove-compartment. She grabbed at his arm.

'What are you doing?'

'What am I doing?' he snarled, shook himself free and took the gun from the glove-compartment. 'I'm going back there.'

She stood directly in front of him, blocking his way, squinting into the sunlight.

'You're crazy. Go back there, we're done for.'

He pushed her aside. 'Shut up! I'm thinking. Listen. He came from this direction but we didn't pass him. That means that the fucker's been watching the chalet. God knows for how long! He must have been holed up in the woods some-where.'

She walked around the car and strapped herself in the driving-seat. He came after her, flushed with rage.

'I've *got* to go back!'

'If you go, you go by yourself. Come on, let's get out of here!'

He moved in beside her and the Jaguar shot down the grade. The sound of its exhaust echoed through the forest. He slipped the gun into his waist-belt, steadying himself as the car slid into a bend. His free hand was resting on the bag behind the seat.

'Easy, Fran. Easy,' he warned. There were pieces of shale on the highway and the rear wheels were firing fragments at the verge.

She showed no sign of having heard. Her face was set and she didn't look at him. The speedometer was nuzzling sixty miles an hour and this was a one-in-four gradient. With *bends*, he remembered. And twenty or thirty more of them still to come.

He heard the noise without surprise, almost as if he had been expecting it, the unmistakable sound of a flat tyre. Fran's face tightened as she fought the car to a halt. He unfastened his seat-belt and was out before she was. The nearside rear wheel was down on its rim.

'Jesus Christ!' he said, looking at it. 'Keys!' She brought them to him hurriedly. Her face showed no fear, no more than a sort of resignation. It was the first time that he had used the jack and he found it awkward. Thankfully there was air in the spare. Fran wedged a couple of rocks under the front wheels and sat down on the sandy bank.

Pastoral, he thought. If she'd driven more carefully he wouldn't be changing a wheel. He used the lug-wrench, the sweat in his eyes and dripping from his armpits. He cranked the chassis high enough to remove the flat, replaced the wheel and lowered the chassis again. Fran was still sitting on the bank, her chin in her hands, watching him. He scrambled up, using the inside of his forearm to wipe his forehead. He threw the spare in the boot.

'OK,' he said, breathing heavily. 'Let's move it.'

THIRTEEN

THE SUNSHINE WAS BRIGHT only a few yards away but it was cool twilight where Raven was standing in the trees, and still, like the interior of a cathedral at midnight. The friable earth was covered with fir-cones and creeping ivy. He was some distance from the road, looking out across the plateau. Trees had been felled or had fallen centuries ago, the rotting vegetation enriching soil irrigated by mountain streams. The scene was like an illustration from a William Tell folk-tale with its dark-green conifers, gentle cattle meandering through long grass and the backdrop of snow-tipped peaks.

The plateau was about a mile long and half as wide. Only one road traversed it. There were no fences, no means of telling who owned which land. The Volkswagen was parked in front of a garage at the side of a small chalet. A track led beyond the chalet to a farmhouse some two hundred yards distant. There was a silo-tower and outbuildings. Smoke was coming from one of the chimneys. A second farmhouse sprawled on the other side of the highway, further away.

There was traffic through the valley and beyond. Raven could see the faded notices flapping on the bus-shelter opposite the chalet. The two men left the Volkswagen, De Wayne walking behind Tyler and still carrying the bag. Someone opened the front door of the chalet from inside and the two men disappeared. Raven slapped hard as something stung the side of his neck. Then again and again, shaking himself furiously. He had been leaning against a tree-trunk and a regiment of red ants was using his wrist as a bridge. He straddled the Honda and rode through the trees to a point that brought him closer to the chalet. He stopped the motor and lit a cigarette. An old con had once explained the thrill of moving through a house at night, unseen and unsuspected, the Invisible Man. It was a feeling that Raven was able to appreciate, to reign supreme in the realm of the hunter. He was glad that De Wayne and Tyler were back together. He had no interest at all in how they had resolved their difference. The end result was simply a neater package. Nor had he animosity for them any longer. After all, they were finally giving him a run for his money.

He jumped as two reports rang out. The trees muffled the echoes but he knew that the shots had come from the chalet. Something moved close to his head. A large owl rose and flew off silently, keeping to the shadows. Raven's eyes were fixed on the chalet. The shots sounded as if they had been fired from the same weapon. Suddenly the front door of the chalet was thrown wide. De Wayne's girl hurried through. She reversed the Volkswagen out on to the road and lifted the garage door. The Jaguar was backed out and left pointing towards the lake.

Raven scratched his bites furiously. De Wayne emerged from the chalet on the run and threw something into the back of the Jaguar. The money without any doubt. He and the woman changed seats and De Wayne drove off. Raven jotted down the number on the licence-plate. Three people had entered the chalet. The one who was left was dead, he was certain of it. Shots and murder, if that what it was, had left no mark on the peace of the plateau. He rode fast down the highway to the chalet. It was smaller than he had thought with an ugly iron-piping fence. At the back were a few neglected flower-beds and some fruit-trees. He tried the front door but it was locked. The windows were shut tight, the curtains drawn. He ran to the rear of the chalet and made his way through the apple-trees, aware that a woman was watching him from the end of the track.

The back door resisted his pressure. He paused long enough at the window to see the body lying on the floor inside. He used the butt of the thirty-eight on the glass, reached through and released the catch and then clambered through into the sink. The kitchen stank of gunfire. Tyler was lying face-down, clothing crumpled, in a pool of blood. Raven jumped down and knelt at the dead man's side, swatting the flies away. He lifted Tyler's head. His eyes were open and staring. Raven straightened up, looking for a phone. There was none in the bedroom, which showed signs of having been slept in. The sitting-room was next to the kitchen, a stuffy room with glass-topped cases filled with dried wild flowers and butterflies hanging on the wall. The telephone was on a side-table. He picked up the hand-set, reading the instructions on its base. POLIZEI. He dialled the first digit before he realised that the line was dead. His eyes followed the cord to its dangling end. He dropped the phone as a shotgun barrel was poked through the window. Bright-blue eyes peered in from a nut-brown face. Then the entire window-frame collapsed under the impact of the farmer's burly body. He came through the space he had made, shedding broken woodwork and splinters of glass. The barrel of his shotgun menaced Raven.

'*Hände hoch!*' he ordered.

Raven's gun thudded to the carpet. He lifted his hands high in the air, realising the difficulty of his position.

'*Un homme est mort,*' he explained urgently. '*L'assassin . . .*'

'*Maul halten!*' roared the farmer. He was a large man with hair like grey barbed-wire and sweat on his face. His boots and corduroy knickerbockers smelled strongly of the farmyard. He kicked the door to the kitchen open, his eyes growing smaller as he saw Tyler's body.

'*Verfluchter schwein, du!*' he bellowed, his expression enraged. He unfastened the back door and gestured outside. '*Marchieren!*'

Raven moved forward gingerly, eyeing the shotgun. The safety-catch was in the OFF position. A track beyond the apple-trees led to a yard flanked by barns and the farm-house. Liquid manure was seeping into a tank and a wall-eyed cat dozed on top of a pile of cow-dung. Hens were scratching the dirt in the barn. Raven picked his way across the farmyard, aware of the woman at an upper window. She had pale flat hair above a frightened face. It was the woman he had seen before, watching him from the end of the track. She dropped the curtain as their eyes met.

The shotgun barrel prodded Raven's spine, urging him forward into the stone-built house. Pans of water were steaming on trivets in front of the enormous kitchen fireplace. Logs smouldered on blackened flags. The long pine table was bare, the chairs surrounding it scrubbed spotless. A ludicrous cuckoo-clock hung above a seedsman's calendar. The telephone was on a dresser against the whitewashed wall. The farmer shoved out his right arm, pointing the shotgun at Raven while composing the digits with his left hand. He spoke excitedly, his sing-song dialect incomprehensible to Raven. But two words were recognisable. 'Emtal' was the name of the hamlet and he knew that '*Todt*' meant either 'dead' or 'death'.

The farmer put the phone down and stood with his back pressed against the edge of the dresser. He was obviously pleased with himself.

'*Ja!*' he said heavily. He wagged his head as though suddenly aware that his listener understood nothing of what he said.

Raven gestured with his uplifted hands. 'Can I put them down?' His arms ached and one language was as good as another. There was no response. He lowered his arms cautiously. The ant-bites were itching and he wanted to scratch yet dared not. The farmer's bright-blue eyes were watchful but he made no demurral.

The open doorway was ten feet away. Beyond that was the track to the highway. It was twelve minutes since Raven had gone through the chalet window. The cuckoo-clock was absurd, its woodwork crudely varnished, its winding-chain flimsy, but it fascinated him. Twelve minutes. Long enough to give De Wayne a five-mile start even on the bends of a mountain road. Raven licked his lips. It was unthinkable to come so close to success and be ruined by a clown with a shotgun. Another couple of minutes' grace and he would have been hot on De Wayne's tail. Cunning replaced his frustration. Explanations would have to wait.

He touched his throat with forefinger and thumb, pantomiming his need of a drink. The farmer had his elbows resting on the dresser, holding the shotgun with both hands in front of him. He opened his mouth and yelled. 'Hannelore!'

His wife's tread sounded on the staircase. She appeared in the doorway, her face fearful still. The farmer spoke to her quickly, watching Raven all the time. She bent at a press and took out a glass, polishing it with the edge of her apron. She held the glass to the light before filling it with water at the tap. Raven moistened his lips again. It was now or never. He ducked under her outstretched arm as she neared him. He came up behind her, holding her tight, his body shielded by her ample girth. The glass smashed on the stone floor. A dog barked outside. Raven swung the woman around and backed away from the shotgun towards the doorway. Reaching it, he propelled her forward with a violent shove, at the same time slamming the door shut.

He ran for the track, zigzagging across the farmyard, awaiting the roar of the shotgun. He was halfway up the track before it came, fired from thirty yards away, the pellets scattered out-of-pattern and harmless. He continued to run, his legs pumping, his elbows tucked in and beginning to labour. Another twenty yards with nothing ahead but the apple-trees and the chalet. The farmer's bellow came from behind but he was no nearer. Raven skirted the iron-piping fence and looked in both directions. The highway was empty. He pulled the Honda upright, threw a leg over the saddle and hit the starting-button. The motor fired and he grabbed his helmet from the handlebars. It was on his head as the farmer burst through the apple-trees, firing his reloaded weapon. Pellets pinged off metal and stone, expending themselves uselessly. Raven was out of range now, clocking sixty miles an hour and leaning low into the first bend. The road ahead unwound, a black shiny snake with a white stripe running its length. He rode with his head down, charged by a surge of adrenalin. They didn't have *that* much start on him. And they'd be running full of confidence, unaware of pursuit. God *damn* that clod with his shotgun and sense of civic duty!

The first task was to get to a phone. Instinct told him that De Wayne would be playing it safe from now on. There would be no rash moves – just an orderly progression to whatever frontier-post he had chosen. He'd be reckoning that there was no need to do otherwise. And that was his weakness. No matter which way he ran he would have to go through police-control. And with any luck they'd be ready for him.

Raven opened his throttle another couple of notches. The wind sang in his ears like violin strings. He hadn't put on his goggles and his eyes were watering. Speed and the wind exhilarated him but the thrill of the chase most of all. The bastards wouldn't escape him now, he was sure of it. The first garage would have a phone.

De Wayne had redistributed the contents of the dispatch-case. He and Fran were carrying a hundred thousand dollars each. The certificates of deposit were in the glove-compartment. He adjusted the gun in his waist-belt. No matter what Raven found he was going to be too late. De Wayne tore up Tyler's Irish passport and flight-ticket, sailing the pieces through the open window as they drove. He bent his head, keeping his eyes on the road, and extracted a cigarette from the pack with his lips. He used the lighter on the dash. Both windows were down, the breeze cool on his face. Only his scalp was uncomfortable, sweat irritating the scab. He sniffed the fingers of his right hand. The smell of burned cordite seemed impressed upon his flesh.

'We'll bury this thing in the city,' he said, breaking the long silence. 'We'll take the first plane out as long as it isn't a domestic flight.' He corrected himself hurriedly. 'Even if it *is* a domestic flight.'

She barely turned her head. She'd taken the wheel again and refused to surrender it. 'You've changed your mind three times since we left the chalet.'

It was true but he had no need of her reminder. 'A princess with a heart of gold,' he said sarcastically.

Her voice was indifferent. 'Another thing. You said you were going to get rid of that gun.'

He spun his cigarette through the window, suddenly sick of it.

Her teeth were the colour of a puppy's, her mouth attractive even when bitter.

'That woman must have heard the shots. And what about Raven?'

'Bullshit!' he blustered. 'They heard a hunter in the forest.' But the thought weeviled into his brain. God alone knew how long Raven had been hanging around. All the guy had to do was look through the window. He should have gotten rid of Tyler's body, dumped it somewhere in the woods. 'You worry too much,' he said obstinately.

'That's great,' she said, her fingers tightening on the steering-wheel. 'Alone in the dark, scared for my life and I *worry* too much!'

He put his hand on her knee. 'Fran, honey, listen. I tell you everything's going to be all right. We're sitting on a couple of million bucks that say so.'

They were out of the pine-woods now. The road had lifted to the level of the grassy slopes that rolled down to the busy lakeshore highway. The giant cutout of the Domecq bull loomed dark against the blue sky. Water sparkled beyond. Suddenly a new sound filled the convertible, the drone of a powerful motor-cycle being ridden at speed. De Wayne twisted his head, looking back through the rear window. The helmeted figure on the machine was a hundred and fifty yards behind but closing the gap between the two vehicles.

'*Shit!*' De Wayne said savagely. He shifted still further

so that he had Raven in full view. Fran put her foot down hard and the Jaguar surged. De Wayne aimed his gun and fired but the shot cracked wide of the oncoming motor-cyclist.

'Stop!' yelled De Wayne. His mouth was bitter and dry. Fran made no reply, increasing the speed of the Jaguar as they hit the last slope down to the four-lane highway. He lowered the gun and released the catch on his door, holding it open, ready to jump. 'Stop the goddam car!' he ordered.

She took her eyes off the road long enough for him to read their implacability. *The bitch didn't intend to stop, not now or ever. She was crazy.* She turned away again, looking straight in front of her from a tight, impenetrable face. He pulled the door shut, his mind jinking like a hunted fox. Raven was sitting bolt upright, maintaining his distance like a traffic-cop cruising the freeway, just out of range.

De Wayne thought of grabbing the handbrake. Then he tried again, pleading as they neared the end of the cut-off. The traffic ahead was heavy, running east and west in front of them. A garage angled the exit, an eight-pump operation with a wash-bay and wide frontage. Cars were parked at the pumps. Fran swung the convertible right on to the garage forecourt. De Wayne dug his feet into the floor-boards as the Jaguar sideswiped its way through the rows of parked cars. She was taking the shortest way out on to the highway. Horns blared from all directions. She found space in the line but only for a second. The car behind nudged their rear, gently at first like a calf butting its mother for milk and then harder. The Jaguar spun away to the left, out of control, taking the dividing rail with it and ploughing into the oncoming traffic. For the Lancia coming towards them there was only one way to go. The two cars met, locked and then crashed. The cherry-trees on the hillside were fat with blossom. It was the last thing that De Wayne saw in his lifetime.

Raven had lost the Jaguar on the last bend before the mountain road joined the highway. The convertible was still out of sight as he neared the garage on the corner. He heard the crash seconds later, the dull crunch of metal against metal followed by the blare of a car-horn. It was all over by the time he wheeled on to the eight-pump forecourt. The Jaguar was lying upside down on the westbound side of the highway, horn stuck and wheels spinning. The soft top had collapsed and there was no sign of movement inside. The driver of a nearby Lancia was throwing up by his wrecked vehicle. More crashes signalled a series of end-to-end pile-ups. The traffic slowed and then halted. People were out of their cars, shouting and gesticulating. A couple of motor-cycle cops had appeared from nowhere and were forcing open the doors of the Jaguar. Then a truck-driver hid them from view, dragging a heavy-duty fire-extinguisher over the hardtop. Tyre marks burned into the road showed the path that the Jaguar had taken.

Raven rolled on a few yards and killed the motor. The doors of the convertible were open now. De Wayne's body was first to be brought out, carried backwards by one of the highway patrolmen. De Wayne's legs trailed as the cop supported him as far as the grass. The second cop carried the girl, her form equally lifeless. A crowd had gathered and was pressing in on the scene of the accident, finally blocking Raven's view completely. He took off his helmet and hooked it over the handlebar. Then he wiped his forehead. Four people had died violent deaths. If he'd gone to the police in the first place, to the Quai des Orfèvres not to Suzini, he might have saved three of their lives. The chase had ended badly and a lot of explanations would have to be made.

A police-siren wailed in the distance, an unmarked BMW preceding an ambulance through the stalled traffic. Raven walked over to the phone-booth next to the garage office. The police would be looking for him by now, alerted by the farmer. The thing to do was to get to headquarters before they found him. His story would come much better that way. He dialled the *Balmoral Hotel*. His room didn't answer according to the girl on the switchboard. He waited while she had Kirstie paged unsuccessfully. He opened the door of the booth, wiping his forehead again, uneasy at Kirstie's absence. It wasn't like her to leave when he had asked her to stay. He needed her there when he did his explaining. The highway-patrolmen had started the traffic rolling in three of the four lanes, their whistles shrill. A sailing-dinghy had bent into the wind, bringing its owner closer to the shore for better inspection of the accident. The Jaguar was shrouded in a cocoon of foam. Raven started to cross the forecourt again, watching the ambulance-doors close on the two bodies. A couple of men stepped from behind the petrol-pumps as Raven neared the Honda. He saw the second police BMW too late. It was parked near the junction with the mountain turn-off.

The plain-clothes men moved professionally, one in front of Raven, the other behind. He made no show of resistance but his arms were pinioned just the same. The detective facing him searched Raven expertly, finding the gun without comment. It was Raven's passport that appeared to interest the officer. He flipped it open and shut before putting it in an inside pocket of his jacket. Handcuffs snapped on Raven's wrists, securing his arms behind his back. A ring of faces peered in curiously as Raven was marched to the parked police-car. The two plain-clothes men settled him between them on the back seat. One of them spoke to the driver, who used the radiophone. He replaced the instrument and took a long look at Raven in the rear-view mirror.

Raven cleared his throat. 'You're making a mistake, gentlemen,' he said in French.

Nobody answered nor was anything more said. The BMW shot forward, changing lanes constantly, the banshee wail of its siren scattering anything that was in its way. Boats were still out on the water. Late-afternoon shoppers crowded the streets of the city. The BMW crossed the bridge by the Rathaus and turned in through high gates that were closed behind them. One of the detectives removed Raven's handcuffs.

'Out!' he said in passable English.

Raven looked around the yard, rubbing his chafed wrists.

This had to be police-headquarters. Plain-clothes men were crossing the yard to the line of powerful BMWs and there was an air of general urgency. His escort led him to a door in the side of the building. A young detective was waiting inside the corridor. He pinned Raven with a no-nonsense look.

'Lauterbach,' he announced. There was something quaint about his formality.

The corridor was wide and sunny with greenery growing in the windows. Raven heard the clatter of typewriters and what sounded like a telex machine. His escort had disappeared. Lauterbach pointed along the corridor. 'You will come with me, please.'

They walked thirty yards and stopped at an open door. Lauterbach stood to one side, motioning Raven forward.

'Please to go in !'

He closed the door quietly behind Raven's back. The room had a blue carpet, well-polished table and upright chairs. A conference room, perhaps. Kirstie was sitting by the open window. Raven swung round on impulse and opened the door again. Lauterbach was standing just outside.

'I'd like my passport back,' said Raven. 'One of those officers has my passport.'

'*Bitte*, inside,' said Lauterbach. This time the key was turned in the lock from the corridor.

Raven opened his arms as Kirstie ran towards him. He held her tightly, looking down into her face. Her hands were digging into his flesh.

'I called the hotel,' he said. 'Where the hell were you? What are you doing here?'

She put her fingers to her lips, looking around her. 'You mean *bugged*?' he said. 'So what?' He took her back to the window. The room overlooked the river with its neat lines of gaily covered boats awaiting use at the weekend. 'Now then,' he said quietly. 'What's going on?'

She shrugged or shivered, he wasn't sure which. 'The police know everything. They must have known some of it even before I came here. I *had* to come !'

He slapped his pockets for a cigarette but they were empty. 'I was going out of my head with anxiety,' she said.

He fished in her purse for a cigarette. 'Right,' he said, exhaling. 'Suppose you tell me just what you *have* done!'

Something in his manner or tone seemed to rile her. 'Jesus God!' she burst out. 'What am I supposed to do, plead guilty to something? It's positively macabre how unfeeling you can be at times.'

He shook his head, more shaken than he cared to show. 'Look, this *is* police-headquarters, Kirstie. I've got a good idea why I'm here. It's you that I'm worried about.'

A boy on the bridge below was fishing off the parapet, his legs dangling precariously.

'They searched the room,' said Kirstie. 'And they took my passport. I've been to the Canadian consul.'

He swung her round so that they were looking at one another. 'Concentrate,' he demanded. 'Try to give me this thing in one piece.'

She took a deep breath. 'They're going to arrest you.'

He wanted to laugh. The expression on her face stopped him. 'They've already done it,' he said. 'The others are dead. All three of them. De Wayne shot Tyler and the girl crashed their car. That's why I'm here, Kirstie. I saw the whole thing.'

She took her fingers away from her throat. 'The French have asked for our extradition.'

'*Extradition!*' His whole body stiffened. 'What in hell are you talking about, Kirstie? Extradition for *what*?'

She made a gesture of impatience. 'I can't . . . maybe it's the wrong word, I don't know. You seem to think that this is some sort of a joke, a game. Well, it isn't. These people are very serious, John. We knew that man in the forest was murdered and we did nothing about it.' She closed her eyes tightly but the tears squeezed past nevertheless.

He walked the length of the room and back. 'How long have they had you here?'

She brushed at her eyes. 'I don't know. I've been here

twice. I've lost track of time. *Please* try to understand. I was desperate. I had to do *something*.'

'Who have you talked to?' he demanded. He used his handkerchief to dry her eyes. He knew her fierce pride and her tears upset him.

'The Commissioner,' she said, and looked in her hand-mirror to repair her face. 'A man called Städelmann.'

He buried his mouth in the palm of her hand. 'I'm sorry, darling,' he said. 'I truly am sorry.'

She touched the back of his neck. Love, worry, frustration – her look showed all of them.

'Just don't be aggressive with him,' she said. 'He's been kind to me.'

The indignity of having been handcuffed was still vivid in his mind. 'Why the hell shouldn't he be kind to you?' he demanded.

'He's trying to help,' she explained. 'He's genuinely trying to help.'

'Good,' he said shortly. 'It looks as if we're going to need it.' He banged on the door. It opened after a while. Lauterbach's scout-master face was impassive.

'I'd like to speak to Herr Städelmann,' said Raven.

Lauterbach showed no surprise. 'The Commissioner is waiting for you. Please, Miss Macfarlane, you will come as well.'

He took them to a large sunny room with a view of the Rathaus. The big man who rose from the desk was wearing a soft tweed suit the colour of peat and glittering rimless spectacles.

'My name is Städelmann,' he announced in perfect English. Lauterbach ducked his head and left the room.

There were two chairs facing the Commissioner. Kirstie took one, Raven the other. He caught a glimpse of his passport on the desk with a buff folder next to it. He recognised its colour and shape. He already had a dossier. The next thing would be to find himself in a cell. He helped himself to Kirstie's cigarettes.

'Miss Macfarlane tells me that we're in some sort of

trouble,' he ventured. It was badly phrased but he didn't know how else to put it.

The Commissioner's shrug was non-committal. 'I'm afraid that I have to agree with her. In your case, certainly.'

Raven looked up over the flaring match. 'I'd like it understood that anything that Miss Macfarlane may have done was at my direction. I want to make it quite clear.'

Städelmann nodded. 'I'd say that is quite clear, Mr Raven. In fact it is evident from the communications we have had from the French authorities.' He opened the folder and read. 'You retired from the Metropolitan Police Force five years ago without completing your term of service, is that correct?'

'You have the wrong word,' said Raven. 'That should read "resigned" and not "retired". I'm sure that your English is good enough to appreciate the difference.' Kirstie's fingers clenched and unclenched. He sensed her nervousness.

Städelmann stared at a patch of sunlight on the wall. 'A bizarre affair,' he remarked. 'Four people dead and an ingenious fraud from which nobody benefits. Except, of course, you, Mr Raven.'

'I don't understand,' said Raven.

'But surely,' Städelmann said mildly. 'The scheme aborted thanks to your actions, misguided though they might have been. Securities were recovered from De Wayne's car. There is no appreciable loss to the banks. The Swiss are practical people, Mr Raven. There will be a substantial reward.' He showed his teeth as if genuinely pleased with the announcement.

'Extradition,' said Raven. 'Kirstie says that the French police are asking for my extradition. Is this correct?'

Städelmann nodded. 'Failure to report a capital crime, aiding and abetting a felon to evade justice. The articles cited in their code approximate roughly to ours.' He spoke with the easy assurance of someone familiar with his subject.

Kirstie leaned forward, brushing the strand of hair from her eyes. 'Mr Raven *isn't* a criminal. He was a police-officer himself and a good one. An *honest* one. That was the trouble.

OK, a man was murdered in that house in the forest but without John the killer would never have been caught.'

'The killer is dead,' Städelmann said mildly.

'Please!' Kirstie's voice was close to breaking. She pulled herself together with an effort, her eyes on the Commissioner. 'Whatever John has done, justice was intended. These people were criminals.'

Städelmann looked from her to Raven and then switched off the tape-machine on the desk. It was neither displayed nor hidden. It was just there and Raven had not noticed it.

'I intend to talk frankly,' said Städelmann. 'There will be no record of anything said in this room. I have to talk frankly because it is clear that neither of you understands the reality of your situation.'

A horn blared outside, the sound disturbing the sudden silence. Raven sat up a little straighter. He found Kirstie's hand and held it, calm for the first time since his arrest. There was no subterfuge in Städelmann's manner, none of the false friendliness that Raven remembered in similar circumstances. Städelmann was sure of himself and of his opinions.

The Commissioner joined his fingers, considering his wedding-ring. 'I respect your record as a policeman, Mr Raven, but much of what I sense in you disturbs me deeply. Switzerland is a small country, independent of political blocs and military alliances. We are like God. If we didn't exist they would have to invent us. To put it plainly, other countries need us. And it is the certainty of rule under the law that makes us attractive. Do you understand what I'm getting at?'

'No,' said Raven.

Städelmann's smile went but his tone remained courteous. 'I'm trying to explain why we want none of your kind of justice. No "cowboys", I believe you call them. People like you with their own ideas about right and wrong.'

Kirstie's hand twitched in Raven's grasp. Städelmann appeared to be awaiting an answer. Raven took a long deep breath.

'I've never been good at making apologies. You have every right to say what you've said and I'm sorry. If I had the time over again I would do things differently. That's all there is to it.' He freed his hand and groped for yet another cigarette.

The Commissioner was pensive, his mouth and chin hidden in his palm. 'This gun,' he said after a while. 'The one that was taken from you. Where did you obtain it?' His eyes were suddenly bright and direct.

'It was Tyler's,' Raven answered, embarrassed by every admission that he was forced to make. 'It's the one he used to kill the Italian.'

Light glinted on Städelmann's spectacles. 'A sordid affair,' he said reminiscently. 'And sordid people. The sort of human beings that one doesn't regret.'

He rose from the desk and went to the window, speaking with his back to them.

'I don't take this French demand too seriously. Nor do they, judging by their wording of their request. I have sent a reply saying that in my opinion an application for extradition would fail in our Federal courts.' He turned to face them.

Städelmann's expression betrayed nothing, but hope jumped in Raven's throat, making speech difficult.

'Does that mean that we're free?' he demanded incredulously.

The big Swiss shrugged. 'That depends what you mean by "free", Mr Raven.' He returned to his desk and produced the two passports. He gave Kirstie hers first. 'There is a flight to Paris in one hour and ten minutes. Two seats have been reserved on it. You can pay at the airport. I suggest that you make your peace with the French.' He glanced at his watch and opened the door to the corridor. Lauterbach was waiting outside.

'Take Miss Macfarlane and Mr Raven to the *Balmoral Hotel*.' The Commissioner offered his quizzical smile. 'Goodbye,' he said and came to the door.

'Goodbye,' said Raven. 'I want you to know that I'm grateful,' he added.

Städelmann nodded. 'There will be correspondence. I shall send it to your address in London. Goodbye, Miss Macfarlane.'

Kirstie gave him her hand. 'I shall remember you, Commissioner. I'll never forget you.'

Städelmann's smile returned. 'You will, young lady. There will be other things to occupy your mind. More important things, thank goodness.' He closed the door gently in their faces. Lauterbach's cough was discreet.

'If you are ready . . .'

'Sure.' Raven took Kirstie's arm. It was cool outside in the yard, with the sun below the horizon. But the air had never smelled sweeter.

>>> If you've enjoyed this book and would like to discover more great vintage crime and thriller titles, as well as the most exciting crime and thriller authors writing today, visit: >>>

The Murder Room
Where Criminal Minds Meet

themurderroom.com

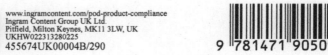